WOLF RANCH: FERAL

WOLF RANCH - BOOK 3

RENEE ROSE
VANESSA VALE

Wolf Ranch: Feral

Cover design: Bridger Media

Cover graphic: Period Images; Deposit Photos: tolstnev

WANT FREE RENEE ROSE BOOKS?

Go to http://subscribepage.com/alphastemp to sign up for Renee Rose's newsletter and receive a free copy of *Alpha's Temptation, Theirs to Protect, Owned by the Marine, Theirs to Punish, The Alpha's Punishment, Disobedience at the Dressmaker's* and *Her Billionaire Boss*. In addition to the free stories, you will also get bonus epilogues, special pricing, exclusive previews and news of new releases.

GET A FREE VANESSA VALE BOOK!

Join Vanessa's mailing list to be the first to know of new releases, free books, special prices and other author giveaways.

http://freeromanceread.com

1

ROB

My best friend and ranch hand Clint slapped me on the shoulder as we made our way up the walk to the front porch of our neighbor's ranch. "Maybe she's cute."

I hadn't been to the Shefield house since the old man passed away. The concrete heaved in spots, and weeds sprouted from the cracks. The place needed tending, and hopefully, the niece, Natalie, would tackle it. It was the second week in August, and snow was known to fall in early September. That seemed downright impossible with the ninety-degree weather we were having. At least the hard storms from last month seemed to have ended.

I gave Clint a look that as his boss and alpha should have made him cower, but he only grinned. "What?"

"Cute? Seriously? Are we back in middle school?" I took off my hat, wiped my brow with the back of my hand, then stuck it back on.

"You thought Brittany Simms was cute. Remember that hard-on you got in the cafeteria? Your eyes glowed so bright it was a wonder the humans didn't notice."

I swore under my breath at the embarrassing memory as I climbed the porch steps.

"I have to wonder if your dick ever got hard again."

I gave him another look. Most of my pack members, especially the guys who lived and worked on the ranch, didn't push their luck with me. Clint and I, though, had been friends since birth, raised in the pack together. Still, I was fucking sick of anyone thinking my dick's prerogatives were their business. If I had to go to one more pack's mating games and deal with the heavy expectations that I leave with one of their she-wolves permanently claimed as mine, I was going to shoot myself.

Especially after what happened last time.

"I don't see a mating bite on any female you've dated, asshole," I grumbled.

"I'm playing the field," he replied, offering a small shrug of his broad shoulder.

"More like playing with yourself," I muttered.

He snorted a laugh. "The difference is I'm not alpha. Much less chance of moon madness hitting me. Plus, no one gives a shit if it does, and they have to put me down when I go feral."

"Being alpha's one thing, but everyone keeping track of where my dick's been and where it needs to go is annoying as fuck."

He studied me, then nodded once. "All we know about Natalie Shefield is that she's in a masters program for music somewhere in California. If she can take care of your problem, then what's the hang up?"

"You know what the problem is. She's human."

My brothers might have been able to mate humans, but I couldn't. I was the alpha of the Cooper Valley pack. My pups had to shift, had to be pure. I, personally, didn't give a shit about this, but I knew others did. The grumbling had begun a few years ago when I crossed age thirty without mating and became high risk for moon madness. As time passed and I had yet to find a mate, the muttering got louder, the concerns grew. My pack respected me, and they didn't want to lose me. I had to ensure the line continued. Find a mate —a *wolf mate*—and breed her.

"That makes her off limits," I countered. "If you think she's cute, then you can have a go."

As he opened his mouth to say something, most likely stupid, a female cry cut through the quiet.

I tensed and looked to Clint. Clint looked at me. His blue eyes widened in surprise then concern. A female in trouble raised every one of a shifter male's instincts to help. To protect. To destroy whoever was a threat.

My hand shot out to try the front door. Unlocked. That made it easy, but I wasn't past kicking it down if needed.

Throwing it open, we stepped into the entry. It looked exactly as it had the last time I'd been in, as if my old friend was still around. Old Man Shefield had handed down his house, furnishings and all.

To the right was a family room with a stone fireplace. To the left, a dining room with an antique table and chairs. Directly in front of us was a central hallway that led back to the kitchen and also a staircase that led to the second floor. It turned to the right at a landing halfway up. I'd never been on the second floor, but based on the size of the house, I had to assume there were four or five bedrooms.

"Take this floor," I told Clint. "I'll head upstairs."

Another cry bounced off the walls. I went up the steps two at a time as my friend headed toward the kitchen.

At the top, I looked left and right. Six doors, all closed. I stilled to use my wolf hearing. I picked up ragged breathing from the right.

Shit. She was hurt, perhaps panicked, judging by the pace of her inhales and exhales.

I stopped in front of the first door. Listened. No.

The second. Again, no.

A whimper came from behind the third door, and I threw it open.

Uh... *well.*

A bedroom. Tan walls. Two windows with cream curtains, wide open to try and cool off the room. A rag rug on the floor beneath a brass bed. None of that caught my attention for more than a quick glance.

No.

It was the woman lying on top of the unmade bed who had my attention. She must've come from the shower because a towel was wrapped around her, and her red hair lay in wet tendrils across the pillow. Her knees were bent, her feet planted on the bed nice and wide, and her hand was between them. She was holding a dildo, and it was crammed nice and deep in her pussy.

I COULDN'T MISS the patch of fiery red curls above that well-endowed toy or the way her slick pussy lips were stretched around the latex cock.

It was big, but not as big as me. Especially not now when I was instantly hard as a fucking rock.

As for Clint's comment earlier, yeah, my dick still got hard. Even for humans.

For her.

I was hot all over and not because of the weather.

Holy. *Fuck.*

She startled and gave a small shriek. Before I could blink, she yanked the dildo from her pussy with one hand, reached up and grabbed a gun from the bedside table. With the agility of a panther, she hopped to her feet and pointed it at me.

Somehow, the towel was still wrapped around her.

I held up my hands. "Whoa there."

"Who the hell are you?"

Even though she was armed, I gave the dildo on the bed a quick glance. It was shiny and slick with her arousal.

Fuck.

I stepped into the room, and she took off the safety.

"Easy." I soothed. "I'm Rob Wolf, your next-door neighbor. We heard you cry out and wanted to make sure you were all right."

"As you can see, I'm fine."

She *was* fine. Her cheeks flushed as red as her hair. Her ragged breaths made her lush breasts rise and fall over the top edge of the towel. Now that she was standing, I could see freckles across her bare shoulders. The taut muscles in her arms and thighs. She wasn't a small thing like Colton's mate, Marina. Natalie Shefield was sturdy, solid, and had a fire in her eyes.

Oh, fuck yes. That was all for me. So was the loaded weapon aimed at my chest. I wasn't worried about being shot, unless it was in the head. Otherwise, it would hurt like hell, but my body would work the bullet out as part of the healing process. Pretty quickly... depending on where the bullet entered, it would pop right out. Still, there were other things I wanted Natalie Shefield to do to me while she was naked besides shoot me.

I took a deep breath to calm myself, hoping not to blow my load in my pants and… Holy. Shit.

Holy fucking shit.

My wolf howled and practically preened.

This woman was my mate.

I just knew. Her scent was masked by soap and shampoo, but it was undeniable. Sweet, tangy and as bright as her hair. It smelled *right*. Familiar, even though I'd never picked up the scent before.

Natalie Shefield, who had no qualms about self-satisfaction, was my fucking mate. She didn't have dainty little toys to get her off. Instead, she went all out.

"Now get the hell out," she said. Her gaze didn't waver, neither did her gun hand.

I heard Clint's footsteps coming down the hall, and I turned around and met him in the doorway.

"Is everything—"

"Look at her and die," I growled with full alpha menace.

His eyes widened at my tone—mostly snarl. He tipped his head to the side to see around me, clearly not understanding what was happening, that I'd just met my fucking mate, but I stepped back and slammed the door in his face. Me in the bedroom with Natalie, Clint alone in the hall.

Turning back around, I faced her.

"You're on the wrong side of that door, neighbor." She wasn't sweet like Audrey. She wasn't sassy like Marina. Hell, no. This woman had fucking attitude.

"Maybe you should tell me why you have a gun next to your bed. Who hurt you?"

The idea of someone scaring her enough for her to need

protection like that had my wolf snarling, ready to rip someone's throat out.

"Said the trespassing neighbor," she countered, raising one red brow.

I took another deep breath. I'd seen how wet she was, but I could scent it too. I'd know her anywhere now, even blind.

"I'm not going to hurt you. Never," I added, my voice fierce. "If you're in danger, if someone's threatening you, I want to know."

She nodded once. "Got it. Now get out."

Yeah, she was pissed. She had a right to be. I'd broken into her house, come upon her in a compromising position, and scared the hell out of her. I was lucky I didn't have an extra hole in my body.

Still… she was my mate, and I didn't want to walk away. Ever.

But telling her what she was to me after one sniff would definitely get me that bullet hole.

"Yes, ma'am." I had the she-devil cornered, and her claws… and weapon were out. It was time to retreat. While it wasn't strange to have a weapon in Montana, it was having one beside your bed while masturbating. I'd find out why she was armed at a time like this then go take care of it for her and bury a body. Then I'd get her beneath me, show her she was mine. "I'll go, for now," I told her, taking a step back.

"Knock next time," she warned.

"I would tell you not to scream so loud, but that would be a crying shame."

Her mouth fell open, and she stared at me. I tipped my hat and left, smirking a little as I went.

I'd met my mate, and she wasn't just cute, she was fucking hot. Passionate. Spirited. Feisty. The fact that she aimed a gun at me only made me practically cream my pants.

I stopped halfway down the stairs with a sudden realization.

Natalie Shefield might be my mate, but she was *human*.

Maybe she should have shot me. It would have been less painful. I was fucked and not with a dildo.

2

WILLOW

COCKY COWBOY ASSHOLE.

Rob Wolf was hot as hell, admittedly, but a total dick. How dare he barge into my house... into my room? I set my gun back on the nightstand. Humiliation made my anger burn as I dropped the towel and pulled on my panties.

Dammit. I came to Cooper Valley, to the Shefield property, to entice the neighbor, but not that one.

The other asshole. Jett Markle.

I stood at my window and watched the two cowboys mount their horses—a delicious sight, not only for the sheer grace of their movements but also for the way their asses filled out their jeans. Well, Rob's ass. I wasn't even watching the other guy.

I wasn't surprised when Rob looked back. I'd just given him an eyeful of my twat stuffed with a vibrator. God, I could just die. I should have shot him. That would have felt good. It would have been messy though. Not just a dead body but explaining it to my boss.

He lifted his chin at me from his saddle. How could he even see me? The sun was reflecting off the pane of glass and should have made me invisible from the outside.

Strange.

He tipped his hat next, a sexy smirk on his rugged face. He didn't seem the least bit bothered I'd aimed my service pistol at him.

Damn hot cowboys in general, but damn him, especially. Although his arrogance was a better response than getting all embarrassed and awkward and running out stammering after my little show or piss his pants at having a gun pointed at him. Not that I believed a man like him had ever stammered or pissed himself. He didn't even blink when he came through the door or when I'd removed the safety. My nipples hardened at the size of his figurative balls. I hadn't seen his actual ones, but I hadn't missed the thick outline of his dick in his jeans. It had gone down his leg! What guy was that big? How'd he walk with that thing? Or ride a horse?

I groaned, my pussy unfulfilled, now considering what it would be like to ride *him* to my finish. That thought made my inner walls clench, and I was hornier than ever.

What the hell was wrong with me? The guy had barged into my house, and I was fantasizing about the size of his dick. Of using it instead of my toy to get off.

I was losing it. The only good news was that I'd hopefully snuffed out his interest. I pulled a gun on him and had been bitchy as hell. Rob Wolf probably wouldn't be coming back. Had he honestly thought I needed protecting? I wasn't sure if I should find that appalling or sweet. It didn't matter either way.

I was here for the job. I had to focus on the investigation. On Jett Markle.

I had to blend in though, and I sure hadn't done that with the welcoming committee from the Wolf Ranch. I grabbed said dildo and went across the hall to the bathroom to clean and sterilize it before tossing it back on the bed. It made no sense to put it away. I'd have to use it again later, this time to ease the ache Rob Wolf brought about.

"Fuck," I whispered, pushing the confrontation away. I'd been in tenser scenes than that. I needed to get a grip. And an orgasm. I groaned at myself.

I still needed to clean out the drawers in the dresser to make room for my things... clothes and not just my small sex toy collection. I was a loner and a woman has needs. As for the rest of the place, I would've liked to clean out the whole house, but I didn't want to overstep. This place wasn't mine. I wasn't Natalie Shefield. I was Willow Johnson, DEA agent.

The real homeowner would arrive when the case was over, and I couldn't very well tell her I'd donated her uncle's things, even though that's exactly what should be done for most of it. The house hadn't been updated since the sixties, and I had to be thankful it was too damned warm to need hot water. The place needed work—a gross understatement—and I'd have to tackle some of it while I was here or else it would seem strange.

I pulled my damp hair up into a ponytail and slipped on a pair of cowgirl boots to go with my jeans and tank top. It was time to meet the neighbor, and not the sexy one. I was cranky because while Rob Wolf was a tall drink of water—as they said in Montana—I hadn't gotten off. He'd interrupted me right before the big finish, and now, I was not only hot but horny too.

Not wanting to go to Markle's place completely unarmed, I slid a small pocket knife into my back pocket. I'd rather take my Glock, but that wasn't an option. A knife I could explain away but not a pistol.

I picked up my cell about to text my boss an update, when he called. Speak of the devil... which made me an *employee* of the devil.

"Johnson here," I answered.

"Yeah, what's your status?" No *hello*, no *how's it going in Montana?*

"I've arrived on location and, ah, settled in." Of course, I didn't quite get to finish that settling in, thanks to Rob Wolf. "I'm about to go to Markle's for a friendly introduction."

"I still don't like it," he grumbled.

It worked out perfectly that Natalie Shefield had inherited the property next door to Jett Markle but had yet to move in, meaning no one in the area had met her. We couldn't have asked for a better setup. Finding someone to replace Natalie, a twenty-six-year-old woman with ties to the state, had been narrowed down to me. Only me. I'd lived in Montana until the day after high school graduation, knew how people rolled around here. Regardless, Vaughn thought sending a female agent alone on a job was a disaster waiting to happen. He didn't have another agent to spare to play house in Cooper Valley, Montana. Honestly, I didn't want anyone cramping my style.

There was one advantage to being female in the DEA. It was, well, being female. I knew from my research that Markle was registered on several dating sites and cut a swath through the eligible women in town. He wasn't going to pass on his pretty new neighbor. A single one, which was the nail in the coffin for me having a partner on this undercover job. It wasn't as if any one of my male colleagues could show a little cleavage and sweet talk his way into Markle's house to look for evidence of drug running.

Getting friendly with him was going to be the easiest and most efficient way to get up in his business. While he checked out my boobs in this snug tank top, I'd check out his place. I didn't want to sleep with the guy—I definitely drew a line there, but I had to keep tabs on him, search his property, and figure out exactly what his connection was with the Colombian drug czar Carlos Murrieta. Getting him to *think* he had a shot of getting in my pants, that was something else entirely.

I rubbed some lip gloss on and applied a little mascara. *Watch out, Markle. Here I come.*

I headed out the back door, noticing the screen door needed the hinges oiled, and followed the path along the telephone line toward Markle's ranch. The hedge fund tycoon-turned-rancher had bought the huge property next door. To the world, he'd retired a billionaire to the quiet life of Big Sky Country. The DEA knew he'd left because he'd lost a billion in clients' money and been fired. Digging had discovered that one of his clients was a shell company for Murrieta. We had to assume he was either hiding in plain sight or a cog in the drug running to Canada.

The county records indicated his property was over a thousand acres, half of it open grazing land with a huge farmhouse, the other half rugged terrain with pine and aspen trees. Plenty of space for bad shit to go down.

Markle had been relentlessly trying to buy the Shefield place since he moved in. According to Natalie, he'd emailed and called her with pitches that varied in nature from dire warnings about the state of the deterioration to offers far exceeding the value to downright threatening, saying he'd be turning her in for every type of county code violation imaginable.

Sure, the place needed updating. I paused in my walk, looked back at the house. It was two story with wood siding painted a forest green. It was faded in spots, and the white window sills and trim needed some scraping, but it was... homey. The roof was shot, the grass overgrown. It looked neglected, which it was. But it wasn't dangerous or against county code. Hell, I didn't think there *were* any regulations way out here. It all led to the fact that Jett Markle was most likely a dick. A retired hedge fund manager on paper but most likely a drug runner who wanted the extra land for some illegal purpose.

When I reached the end of my property line, I carefully pulled up the top string of barbed wire and set my boot on the lower one, then slid between them to emerge on his side.

A group of cows turned their heads to watch me approach, completely uninterested. Two were lying down in a small patch of shade near the fence line.

I breathed in the Montana air—the scent of wild grasses and dusty earth hit my nostrils. I'd thought I would hate being back in Montana, but it was strange—there was definitely a sense of "home." A rightness or belonging, even after the nightmare of my childhood. I couldn't hate an entire state for the wrongs of the Carp family. I'd stayed away long enough, but now... I hadn't realized how much I'd missed it. Like this was how outdoors should feel, with the hot sun on my face, the constant breeze, the verdant smell. It was like my body recognized it here over the places I'd been living the past ten years.

I was playing a part, but even the cowgirl boots and jeans felt right on my body. I wished I had the hat to go with the outfit. I made a mental note to buy myself a cowgirl hat at the seed and feed in town. I walked until I neared the ranch house, barn and stable—all new buildings in pristine condition. It made the Shefield place look like something out of a horror flick.

Two men stood near the stable, one of them speaking in a raised voice like he was giving the younger man a dressing down.

Markle. Even if I hadn't spent the last six months investigating the hell out of the guy, I'd know him by the designer jeans and five thousand dollar Stetson that just looked stupid on him. He looked like a Hollywood cowboy. Not because he was good looking, which he was, but because he appeared to be in costume or playing dress-up. He might own a ranch, but he sure as hell wasn't a rancher.

Not like the ones I'd been raised by anyway.

I strode up, and the older man broke off his tirade. Both men gaped at me in surprise.

"Afternoon, gentlemen." I let my hips swing as I approached, and their gazes tracked the movement. When I reached them, I stuck my hand out to Markle. "I'm Natalie, your new neighbor. I wanted to stop by and introduce myself. We... uh, talked on the phone, but that's not the same thing as seeing someone in person." I took the moment to look Markle over, just as he did me. Blatantly, as if I liked what I saw. Dark hair, fake tan, chiseled jaw.

Markle's dark eyebrow raised. Then he grinned, showing off perfect veneers. He was attractive. I wasn't blind and could see women giving him a second look, especially with his vast amounts of money. But he hadn't spoken yet. What was the saying? *Light traveled faster than sound because some people seemed bright until you heard them speak.*

"Yes, in person is a hell of a lot better."

He waited a beat before reaching out to shake my hand. A gold Rolex flashed on his wrist. Definitely out of place on a rancher. He closed his fingers around mine and squeezed too hard. It was the kind of grip that made me want to shake my hand out afterward. Or maybe that was just because I didn't like him.

I didn't let it show, though. I stepped in a little closer and bent down to swat an imaginary bug off my leg, letting him get a view of my cleavage.

He coughed a little, like the sight disturbed his equilibrium. "Jett Markle." He didn't bother to introduce his ranch hand.

I turned my sweetest smile on the other man and stuck out my hand. "Hey, there. I'm Natalie."

"Jack." He gave me a handshake as limp as Markle's was firm and didn't make eye contact. He couldn't be older than twenty, barely old enough to shave. Markle probably had his ranch full of guys he could kick around. He definitely was a power trip kind of guy.

Strange that he was most likely in bed with a drug cartel. It almost seemed like something he'd find beneath him, a task he didn't want to get his callous-free hands involved in. So either the reports of his firing had been wrong, and there was a lot of money in it for him, or he was in bed with them in some way I haven't figured out. Maybe a family connection or more likely Murrieta had something on him.

It was my job to figure it out, so I turned my smile back on Markle and started up my helpless female charade. "I just got in today. You were right on the phone. There's a lot of repairs required. It sure looks like I'll have my hands full."

He eyed me up and down, as if he wanted to have *his* hands full of me. "You have a plan for managing the numerous repairs? Contractors? Funding?"

I grinned back at him. The sun was in my eyes, and I really wished I'd had that cowgirl hat, but this look was probably better, anyway. Let him get a gander at my girl-next-door freckles and youthful appearance. Let him underestimate me. I knew he was thirty-five, so he might even play the daddy card if he got off on it.

"No, I'm just going to try to tackle things on my own."

I saw calculation in his eyes. "Well, I might still be willing to take a piece of your land. You'll probably be desperate for cash for the repairs. I know the county taxes haven't been paid yet."

Yeah, the asshole was probably hoping to buy the lien on them the moment it came up at auction. I'd have to let the real Natalie know she was in danger of losing the property for a few thousand bucks of unpaid taxes.

I tipped my head to the side. "Thanks for the offer. I'll take it into consideration." I made my voice soft and husky while I tried not to clench my hands into fists, ready to punch him in the face. What a dick.

The sultry tone worked. The hardest edge of him softened. "You probably don't have your kitchen stocked yet or even the utilities turned on. How about I take you to dinner in town tonight? Show a little local hospitality."

Markle considered himself a local. That was hilarious.

I feigned consideration, biting my lip. "Yeah, I guess that would be nice. I don't have much in the house. But only if you promise not to try to wear me down on selling the place. As I told you before, it has a lot of sentimental value to me."

"All right." He scratched the back of his neck as if those words cost him. "I'll pick you up at seven."

I glanced at Jack, who hadn't said a word, then nodded. "Deal. I'll see you then."

I put a little promise in my voice but not too much. I

didn't want to have to screw the guy or kick him in the nuts on our first date. I was trying for an opening to be on his property and get to know his habits and schedule. Dinner was a warmup and a way in, which meant I could stop back again, especially if he thought he had a chance to get in my pants.

I left the way I came, knowing the men were watching me—most likely my ass—as I sauntered away.

All right, I was in.

First objective achieved.

Tonight I'd do my part to ingratiate myself to the target next door. After I got home, I would finish what I started. Not because I'd picture him to get off but because all the time I was taking in Markle, I was comparing him to Rob Wolf. I doubted Markle had a dick that ran down the inside of his thigh. My pussy clenched at the thought. Yeah, I'd be getting off later thinking about my sexier neighbor because I had a feeling after I got a guy like Wolf inside me, I'd be ruined for all others, including my dildo.

3

ROB

BOYD PULLED up in his pickup truck and whistled. He might be my little brother, but I flipped him the bird through the upstairs window. I finished tucking my shirt in. I'd just showered and changed for the pack meeting.

It was the new moon, so a good time to discuss business or resolve any disputes. A time when wisdom prevailed instead of the hot-headedness and passion of the full moon. Especially mine. Every full moon was hell, my wolf pushing me to mate. I ran and ran hard. Thank fuck, I'd been able to run with Colton last time. He'd been worse off than me, pushing me almost past my endurance. It had helped. I could focus now, be the alpha the pack expected.

I went downstairs and out to the truck, setting my hat on top of my damp hair. "Get some fucking manners. You don't whistle for me like a goddamn dog," I said as I climbed in. He drove on to the bunkhouse, the windows down.

Boyd actually did have manners but also made a second career out of deliberately pushing me by showing disrespect. I was sure having a big brother who became both a pseudo-father and pack alpha when we were both still kids ourselves was scarring. He'd played the rebellious playboy role for years until he miraculously met his mate while on the rodeo circuit. As fate would have it, she was a doctor here at our hospital. So thanks to Audrey, he'd come home. Permanently.

As for Colton, he'd mated Audrey's sister, Marina. Small fucking world. He'd just retired from the military, and they were working their way back across the country from his base now. Soon enough, the three Wolf boys would be settled on the ranch again, and a new generation would begin. Audrey was already expecting a pup. Except I wasn't settled, not like they were. Not like it was expected of me, which was a threat to the pack. Which made me pissy about this meeting because there was always talk about the fact that I hadn't mated. Again, my dick was everyone's worry.

Boyd whistled again then gave me one of his signature easy grins. "Well, you came faster than the rest of the dogs."

"Careful, it'll be hard to drive with your eye all swelled up," I warned. Physical retribution was the norm in wolf packs. It was pretty harmless since our bodies healed so quickly.

Despite my grumblings, I had to admit it was nice to have my brother back. I'd been running the pack on my own for long enough. Colton had enlisted right after high school and left for boot camp that same summer. Two years later, Boyd had headed to the rodeo circuit at eighteen. I'd been running the pack alone for a dozen years. It felt good to have my own blood beside me for a change.

The heir and the spare were back. Although, they'd

mated humans. The pack was fine with it because they weren't leading. Everyone looked to me for a *true* wolf match and future alpha.

I thought of the hot as hell neighbor and her greedy pussy. My wolf thought of fucking her hard and biting her deep. My dick hardened, and that was a problem in more ways than one.

Clint came out of the bunkhouse and climbed into the back of the huge pickup. Boyd headed up the back road toward the mountain. He lived that way in a cabin with Audrey, but we were going past that. The pack owned a lodge house up there built by my great-great-great grandfather Makelin Wolf, the founding pack alpha when Montana was still a territory. It was a place where the pack could meet, shift and run far from the prying eyes of humans.

"So Alpha, going to tell us about why you slammed our neighbor's bedroom door in my face?" Clint asked.

He was sitting behind Boyd, so I glanced back at him. Glared. We hadn't spoken of it earlier when we rode back from the Shefield house. He could've asked me about it then, but no. He had to fucking do it with Boyd around.

"*Bedroom* door?" Boyd repeated, steering around a turn.

Clint was my best friend. Boyd was my brother. They were the closest things to confidants I had. I couldn't share all the details of being alpha. Some information was confidential. Like a priest but without the god. My pack members might be able to have secrets but not me. With the way Clint grinned, he had a pretty good idea of what it was. I hadn't acted like that before. Ever.

"Rob," Boyd said, snapping me out of my thoughts.

"We went over to introduce ourselves to the new neighbor."

He nodded, then took his hat off, stuck it on the

console between us, and ran a hand through his fair hair. It caught the wind and blew around. He took after our mother while Colton and I were dark like our father had been.

"You're a man grown, you don't have to be ashamed you were hot for her," Clint prodded. "It's not like we think you're a virgin."

I glanced back at him. "I didn't fuck her."

"But you want to."

"She seemed nice when I talked to her on the phone," Boyd said. "Level headed. Not one to fall for Markle's shit, thankfully."

"She screamed. Isn't that right, Rob?"

"She screamed?" Boyd repeated, glancing my way, then back on the narrow road.

"Tell him why. I mean, it's not like I ever found out."

I growled then, letting the full force of my wolf let him know I wasn't happy with his pettiness.

Of course, that didn't make him cower like it should have. It made him laugh.

"What the fuck was wrong with her?" Boyd asked. "Should Audrey go see if she needs help?"

I ground my back teeth together. What Natalie had been doing had been private. She hadn't even meant for me to witness her pleasure. But I had. And because I had, I'd discovered she was my mate. That was completely fucking untrue because if she were outside sipping lemonade in jeans and a t-shirt, I'd still have picked up her scent and known she was mine.

Fate had intervened though. I learned she was passionate. I learned she wasn't shy about her sexuality. She'd been surprised a stranger had burst in on her, but she'd been more pissed than ashamed. She hadn't hidden that huge dildo but left it on the bed between us, proof of what she'd been doing.

Her cries of pleasure—which we'd mistaken for sounds of pain—weren't those of fulfillment. She hadn't come, which meant she either got busy with her toy again after I left or she was out there, horny and eager for a big dick.

I'd also learned she'd been pleased with what she'd seen in me. Women had said I was handsome, but I hadn't given a shit. I only wanted my mate to be hot for me. When she caught sight of my hard-on… she'd been eager. Wide eyed, which meant no guy had given it to her like I would.

I was hard now and had to shift in my seat.

"Jesus," Boyd said. "What the fuck's going on with our new neighbor?"

I had to tell them. What Clint suspected. What I knew.

"She wasn't hurt." I gritted my teeth some more, said the words I wanted to keep private between me and Natalie. "She was on her bed masturbating."

Boyd grinned. "That must've been a sight."

"He told me he'd kill me if I looked at her," Clint said, leaning forward and patting Boyd on the shoulder. "All growl."

Boyd's brows went up, and he looked my way again.

"Why's that, Alpha?" Clint prodded.

"Natalie Shefield's my mate. I knew the second I breathed in her scent."

Boyd honked the horn, once, then again, then whooped. "Fuck, yeah!"

I slapped my hand on the dash, glared at him. "This isn't good news, Boyd. I can't have her."

He sobered, pulled up in front of the lodge, then turned off the truck. "She's your mate. You've been waiting for her all this time. You *can* have her."

I took off my seatbelt. Sighed and looked up at the building where the meeting would begin shortly. "She's human. I'm pack alpha. Pack members are going to lose their shit if I claim her."

Boyd looked at me with a serious expression, the first one I'd seen on him in a while. "You're going to lose your shit if you don't."

4

ROB

BOYD AND CLINT didn't say anything as we met up with the other guys. Levi, Johnny, Rand and Nash had been the first to arrive. They'd opened the wide doors to let the fresh air in, then we joined them cleaning—sweeping out the month's worth of dust and setting up chairs. Within a few minutes other vehicles arrived, parking along the narrow dirt road or among the trees on either side. Some—especially those who lived up in the mountains—would arrive in wolf form, shifting and changing into clothes they stored here.

I stood in the doorway and formally greeted the adult pack members, shaking hands and reciting their names much like a human church elder would. The children ran off to play in the woods together, just as I had with Boyd, Colton, Clint and the others when we were young.

After my parents died, I used to dread these meetings.

Being thrust into the role of alpha, the one my father had fulfilled in a way I never could, made me think I was less. It had taken me years to realize I was not him and couldn't lead like him. Even so, some doubted. Sometimes I still did, about myself. Especially lately with the elders pressuring me to mark a female, even one who wasn't my chosen mate, just to avoid moon madness. Of course, there wasn't a lot of proof that it worked. I could be mated to a female who I didn't have the urge to mark and still go mad, or so I'd heard.

And now I'd fucked it up even more, my wolf wanting a human for a mate. No one else had appealed to the wolf. Not one. One scent of Natalie Shefield, and I was fucked.

I wanted what my parents had shared. A connection. A deep bond. Chemistry. Love. I wanted my wolf happy. Hell, I wanted to wake up beside my true mate every morning. Content.

I had a responsibility to the pack to carry on the Wolf line, love or not. I held off, month after month. Year after year. For how much longer? My ranch hands and now Boyd always flanked me, showing they had my back like a king's guard. They were all brothers to me. We grew up together. Learned to shift and hunt together. Went to school down in the valley together. Two of them knew the truth, the one thing that could strip me from control, could tear our pack apart.

Clint's parents arrived and greeted me almost reverently. They'd been our guardians when my parents had died. It had been in their will that Tom and Janet take care of us if something happened. Which it had when I'd been only sixteen. For two years, Boyd, Colton and I were under their protection in the eyes of Montana law, but even so, I had been the alpha. *Their* leader. That had held more power than anything the state could dictate.

Janet carried a casserole dish that smelled delicious for the potluck.

"I sure hope that's your meat lasagna," I said, my mouth already salivating for her cooking. She'd had to feed five hungry teenagers... the three of us plus Clint and his younger brother, Rand. Not only did she know what got our butts into chairs around the dinner table every night, she had the calmness of a mother who'd seen it all.

"Of course, it is. Garlic bread, too. I know what you like, Alpha Wolf." The short, thick-waisted woman beamed up at me as she bustled past to set the dish in the kitchen in the back.

Tom thumped me on the shoulder as we clasped hands. They lived nearby in the mountains and were respected elders of the pack. Besides taking care of us, they'd helped us keep the ranch going on our own and offered gentle encouragement as I stepped into my role at far too young an age.

Karen Clifton, one of the unmated females in the pack, arrived next, wearing short-shorts and a tank top. She'd been shoving her tits under my nose for as long as I could remember. I thought she'd have given it up at some point since I'd never indicated a hint of interest, but as long as I remained unmated, I was fair game in her book, especially since she hadn't been able to land one of my brothers before they found their mates. She waved a pie under my nose. "Peach. Your favorite."

It wasn't my favorite, and I wasn't nice enough to even pretend. Now that I'd scented Natalie, Karen was even more repugnant. Her own smell, oddly of almonds mixed with the sickly sweet aroma of sugared peaches, was cloying. My wolf practically snarled at her boldness. I hadn't forgotten how she'd tried to drive Boyd and Audrey apart, either.

I ignored her and reached to shake hands with her father and her younger brother, James, the teen Jett Markle had shot in wolf form earlier this summer. To cover up the incident with the human, Boyd had told Markle he'd shot our dog not a wolf, and Boyd had blackened Markle's eye for it. It wasn't the last run-in we had with the annoying neighbor since then, and I expected more. Once an asshole, always an asshole.

And shit, he was pushing for the Shefield property, which meant he'd be paying a visit on Natalie, too. I tensed, not wanting the fucker anywhere near my woman. What if he'd shown up when Clint and I had?

Boyd set his hand on my shoulder for a second. I nodded. He'd sensed my tension but couldn't ask if I was okay. Everyone here had incredible hearing.

An unfamiliar black pickup parked, and I growled.

"Easy, Alpha," Nathan Brown said, approaching. The elder, who'd been loitering on the wraparound porch, dropped an unwelcome hand on my shoulder. Unlike Boyd's reassuring gesture, this was placating. Patronizing.

He was a few inches shorter, with thinning hair that was turning from brown to gray. He had the paunch of a wolf who didn't run with the pack. "Those are my kin from the Madison Range pack. They were visiting, so I invited them to our meeting. We don't have anything to hide, do we?"

Another low growl rumbled in my throat. Out of the corner of my eye, I saw Clint stiffen, but remain in place.

Yeah, I had nothing to fucking hide.

Bringing extended family to pack meetings was done on occasion, so technically Nathan hadn't done anything wrong, but usually it was with advanced notice out of respect. He hadn't done it this time. I didn't like it. I didn't like it, and I didn't like him.

He was the type who would stab me in the back if he thought he could become alpha. A weasley, slippery type. He'd always been a thorn in this pack's side. The kind who always caused dissension and trouble. I couldn't kick him out for being disagreeable, but with Boyd and Colton back, there was no chance in hell he'd ever become alpha. With Audrey pregnant, the line would continue... if the pup could shift.

"A heads up would've been appreciated," I grumbled.

Some of these guys had been testing me since I was sixteen. Every fucking day. Maybe that's true of any alpha. I wouldn't know. I'd been barely old enough to even take part in pack meetings before my dad died, and back then, I hadn't paid much attention. I'd gone from fucking around with my friends in the back row to standing before everyone.

I kept my eye on Brown's kin as they approached. They had *redneck* written all over them, complete with mullets, heavy metal t-shirts and thick necks. Not that half my pack —especially the ones who lived up in these mountains and rarely interacted with humans—weren't also a little hillbilly. Only good thing about pack politics and having to deal with ignorance and closed-mindedness was that it wasn't a fucking democracy.

I was alpha, and I'd grown into the role. No one fucked with my pack, even from the inside. Everyone felt my alpha power when I pulled it out. They instinctually responded to my commands.

There were four of them—one shifter in his forties, two in their early thirties and a younger wolf—barely an adult.

They had a casual way about them, but I sensed they were on their best behavior.

"Sal Brown," the oldest says to me, extending his hand. I supposed he looked familiar from pack exchanges and mating games we'd had in the past. He wasn't their pack's alpha, but a brother or something.

"Alpha Wolf," I answer coolly, shaking his hand. My name was irrelevant. My title said it all.

"Yeah, I guessed that much." He gives a mirthless chuckle. "Oh right, your *name* is Wolf." The joke sounded rehearsed, one I'd heard about a million times.

In fact, my grandfather used to say, "I'm Alpha Wolf because I'm alpha wolf."

I'd often thought my family was foolish to keep the name Wolf when we, as a species, were trying to blend into human society, but it was a source of pride. We were related to the oldest Wolf families across the globe, and the name was always synonymous with alpha. It wasn't changing now either.

I stared him down, waiting for some explanation about why the fuck he and his crew were at my pack meeting. When it was clear by his hesitation he didn't want to give me one, I released his gaze and let him step inside. His other three family members also introduced themselves and skulked in.

I'd find out the truth, but sometimes the direct approach wasn't the way to go.

"Hi, Alpha. Hey, Boyd." Shelby, one of the few single females came up the steps and smiled. Boyd had taken position at my shoulder when the Brown clan arrived. I'd seek his counsel later on what he thought of them and why they were here.

We didn't shake Shelby's hand because both were full

with a giant glass carafe filled with her famous watermelon lemonade. She was in her late twenties and the full package —pretty, smart, friendly. I never had any interest, though, and fortunately, she hadn't seemed to want me, either. In fact, she'd made it plain she believed in fate and hoped to find her true mate someday, much to the irritation of her mom, who'd been trying to throw us together from the moment she turned eighteen.

My wolf hadn't shown any interest in her or anyone else. I sighed. Until earlier. Until Natalie Shefield. *The human.*

"Shelby," I said, tipping my hat.

I had no idea why Shelby brought my mind careening back to my new neighbor. The vision of Natalie working that dildo and moaning had been ricocheting around in my head all afternoon. The memory of her scent—so sweet and right.

The need to get back to her house—to see her again and find out every detail I could about that bold little redhead—consumed me.

I waited outside until everyone had arrived and then went in and took my position at the head of the circle. Boyd sat on one side of me, with Clint on the other. Rand and Nash took seats by Clint. Johnny and Levi next to Boyd. I was flanked by my inner circle—the ones I'd trust with my life.

I tried to keep the meetings short—for my own sanity, mostly. I didn't have any business to address this month, so I opened the floor.

There were a few minor issues brought up and handled. I was a man of few words, and I didn't tolerate a shit ton of talk at my meetings. Things got solved fast.

"All right. Anything else, or can we eat?" I looked around, eager to get to Janet's lasagna.

"Yeah, I've got something." Nate Brown stood. He looked around the room, addressing the pack instead of me. "I've been wondering when someone was going to mention the latest pack news."

My upper lip curled. A growl started to tickle behind my nose. When I said I'd find out what the guy was up to, I knew the time would come. It seemed to be now. In front of the entire pack.

"What's that?" I snarled.

"I'm surprised you didn't mention it tonight. Namely, how your brother broke pack law by mating a human. And now I hear Colton has mated her sister. Is that true?"

Boyd was on his feet in a flash.

"Sit down," I said in a low growl to him, throwing out my hand. I didn't take my glare off fucking Nate Brown's treacherous face, though. I saw now why he brought his kin. For backup. They probably fueled his previously unvoiced arguments.

"My brothers' mates were approved by their fucking alpha, end of story." I infused my voice with alpha command, causing the whole room to draw a breath at once. "The entire pack was invited to Boyd and Audrey's wedding down at the barn by the big house—it wasn't news. It's over and done. No reason to discuss."

A pup in the back of the room started crying in her mother's arms at the blast of aggression I'd sent out.

"But Colton mated a human, too."

I nodded. "He did." I'd already explained myself enough. Those two words were all he was going to get on the topic.

"Alpha, with all respect," *—bullshit—* "you have yet to choose a mate. At your age and with your alpha power, you are treacherously close to moon madness. What happens to this pack when you have to be put down? Your brothers aren't fit to lead with human mates. And our pack's alpha lineage will die. That'd be a travesty."

The pack members either sat quietly waiting to hear my answer or were whispering between themselves. This had been brought up before but not in such an in-your-face manner. Why him? Why now? He didn't seem the type to be worried I was going to die soon. He had an agenda here, a deeper reason than just sowing discontent.

Boyd growled beside me. Before I could answer, Nate's kin stood up.

"We'll take you." He opened his arms to the pack. "I spoke to my brother, our alpha with the Madison Range pack." Since he'd told me where he was from at the door, he added that for everyone in the room. Which meant this had all been planned. "He'd be happy to absorb the pack when your alpha goes mad. In fact, he'd insist on it."

What. The actual fuck?

This was a goddamn coup. I shouldn't have been surprised, but fuck. Just what I needed right about now. Or ever.

I stood. As soon as I did, Boyd, Clint and every one of my ranch hands surged up around me, all of them growling. Now Clint and Boyd could understand the depth of my problem with Natalie.

"Get out," I snarled, pointing at the door.

Sal Brown raised his brows in mock surprise, like I was being rude for revoking hospitality. "We came in peace. Your pack's in trouble, and we want to help. As a friendly neighbor."

"Get. The. Fuck Out. *Now.* Before I tear you to shreds."

The baby in the back wailed so loudly, her mother took her out of the lodge house through the kitchen. One by one, other men in my pack stood, folding their arms across their chests. They might wonder about my delay in mating, but they were behind me.

The outsiders stood and made their way to the door.

"You too, Nathan." I tipped my head for him to follow. "Get the fuck out."

Nathan hesitated. He'd gone a little pale. The guy's balls most likely had already shriveled at the sound of my alpha command, and now he was probably worried he was out of my pack for good.

He might just be. The fucker would have to make it right with me, but if he tried right now, I was likely to bloody the guy.

Silence descended. I didn't speak or move until I heard two vehicles start and drive away. Then I looked around at everyone who remained, silent and watchful.

"Anyone else here want to say something about my brothers' choices in mates?"

Or mine?

Something sharp and painful twisted in my gut, thinking of how happy Boyd was with Audrey, his pup in her belly. And Colton, pushed to the brink with his own moon madness, but now mated to the woman who was meant to be his. And me?

My wolf had met its mate. For the first time ever, I knew. Just like Boyd and Colton had. One look, one whiff of Audrey's and Marina's scent, and they were fucking goners.

Natalie Shefield, that gorgeous human neighbor of mine. Her scent called to my wolf. Her body called to my dick. Her feisty, brave determination called to my mind.

I'd barely spoken with her. Barely seen enough of her body to satisfy my basest instincts. And yet, she was my mate.

If I'd clung to one shred of hope, I might be able to have

her. It just fucking went up in flames. No way would Nathan or anyone in the Madison Range pack think twice about getting rid of me as alpha if I admitted I had a mate who was human.

This pack was a disaster, and it was all because of me.

5

WILLOW

Mother. Fucker.

I'd just stripped out of my clothes to take a shower after my date with Markle, and the asshole was knocking on my door again. Seriously? I didn't play up the yawning and I'm-so-tired thing at the end of the date enough? I even let the asshole have a kiss before he left me at the door. Denying him that would have hurt my investigation. But even on assignment, I needed to clock out. Sure, I was pretending to be Natalie Shefield, but it was harder pretending to like Jett Markle.

The date had gone fine. I didn't learn much about him of importance, even though he barely shut up the entire time. He had nine hundred acres and planned to build a stable to stud horses. He'd also just purchased a bull to inseminate his cows. When he'd said that, he'd raised a brow, as if he wondered if I needed to be inseminated. By him.

I learned about cattle and the solar panels he'd installed. I'd asked after his time in New York, hoping to learn more about his job and how he no longer had it, but all I'd gotten was a lesson in bond trading.

It had been painful, but it was a start. Maybe I'd smiled and feigned more interest than his previous dates because he'd definitely thought he was going to score.

Now it seemed he didn't know when to stop.

I debated putting my clothes back on, but he wasn't staying long, barely long enough to tell him I had a headache and was just about to wash my hair then shut the door in his face. I threw on my short silky robe and tied it at my waist. Just to be safe, I grabbed my Glock and carried it downstairs, tucking it under a basket by the front door before I swung it open, a slight scowl in place.

And my nipples went hard as diamond points.

Rob Wolf. At my door. Wearing a furious scowl of his own.

"Well. You have a habit of showing up at the worst times," I told him. Although the truth was, after a date with Markle, Rob's large real cowboy form was a delicious sight. As attested to by my nips.

"You armed?"

Those two words gave me goosebumps. Yes, it was ridiculous, but the deep timbre of his voice set me off. I glanced down at myself. "Where would I hide a weapon?"

"You had on a towel earlier," he countered, his gaze raking down my body.

I couldn't help but roll my eyes. "No gun on me."

He understood what I didn't say and looked around for a weapon. Smart man.

He took off his hat, which showed his dark hair was long on top with a curl to it. A little wild, just like him. His scowl grew deeper, and he rubbed the back of his neck. "Tell me you didn't just kiss Jett Markle on this porch," he demanded.

I narrowed my eyes. "Tell me what business it is of yours."

"Fuck." He clenched his jaw like he was grinding his back teeth. I seriously didn't know what his problem was, but he definitely was wound up. "You—" he spluttered then stopped, like he had no idea what to say next. "You have a gun, that's good." He paced a step on the porch then pivoted, like he was trying to work something out. The summer sun had just set, but I could still see him clearly. "I'm sure you think you can take care of yourself, but, dammit, Natalie, that man is trouble." He lifted his eyes to mine, and they were burning with conflict.

Aw.

I shouldn't have been so touched by his concern. Of course, he was probably over here because he'd thought he was going to be the guy getting into my pants. Now he was pissed it was Markle.

Although he did seem genuinely distressed for my safety, not just butt-hurt. Yeah, he'd burst into my house and into my bedroom, but he'd heard me scream. And now he was on my doorstep again—this time he knocked—because he thought I was... what, in danger?

Maybe he knew something about Markle.

Dammit. Now I wished I had gotten dressed because I couldn't exactly invite him in wearing my robe. The last time we'd met I'd been in a towel. This was getting ridiculous.

I leaned my hip against the doorframe. "Trouble how?" I asked, crossing my arms over my chest.

Rob shook his head with frustration. "The bad kind." His nostrils flared like he could smell Markle's cloying cologne on my skin, and he frowned deeper. But that was impossible. Sure, I could smell it on my face because the guy had kissed me, but I'd taken off the clothes that carried the scent. His cologne alone made me hate the guy.

"He shot my dog," Rob blurted, like his mind had just arrived on evidence of Markle's evil. "When you wouldn't sell, he cut your fence and let his cattle in to graze on your land anyway. You heard all that from my brother, Boyd. Believe me, if he's showing interest in you now, it's only because he's gonna look for some angle to not only screw you but screw you out of what belongs to you."

I stepped out onto the porch with him, not because it was a good idea, but because my body seemed to want to be closer to his. "Uh huh. What about you? I seem to recall Boyd made an offer for the land, as well. Markle took me to dinner and didn't get the show that you got earlier. Maybe you're here because you've got plans, too."

Rob had gone still the moment I came close, like a predator preparing to pounce. His gaze was locked on mine, and the intensity in his eyes was no longer frustration. It was heat. "Oh, angel." His voice was soft and low. He stepped forward, closing the distance between us. "My plans for you have nothing to do with your land."

"Then I guess it has more to do with what you saw earlier?" I cocked my head, letting my lips curve at the edges.

His gaze raked down to the peaks of my nipples through the thin robe, then to the hem, which ended far above my knees.

He pressed his hand against his dick, which visibly ran down the inside of his thigh. Oh damn. Was that all for me? I was pretty sure my eyes widened. I knew my lips parted. He was as huge as I remembered.

A smirk formed on his mouth when he observed my reaction to his rather noticeable interest.

"And what I heard." The roughness of his voice had smoothed into dark velvet. "I won't ever forget the way you sound and how you look when you're getting fucked. It's a good thing it was a toy you were playing with because if it was some other guy and his dick was in you, I'd have to kill him. Tell me, angel, did you finish after I left?"

In the porch light, his eyes took on an uncanny glow.

Slowly, I shook my head. "No. You killed the mood." If I didn't sound so breathless, my words might've been the wet blanket I intended.

Oh, who was I kidding? I did want to ride this cocky cowboy. I'd been denying it all day. Yes, it was crazy to have the hots for the guy who broke into my house. Usually, I arrested someone who did that. But I wasn't a DEA agent with Rob. I was just a woman who had needs. There wasn't anything wrong with having them scratched by him.

"Good." The syllable came out as pure satisfaction.

"Good?" I put my hands on my hips, which had the unfortunate effect of loosening the sash on my robe and parting the V at my chest.

Rob groaned, staring at the exposed curves like a starved man. "Yeah, good," he rumbled. "The next time you come it will be beneath me."

"Oh really?" I shot out, but my mouth stretched into a reluctant grin. My bare pussy slickened, moisture leaking onto my inner thighs at how bossy he was. I didn't like bossy men. They annoyed me. But Rob? I loved it although I wasn't going to let him know that.

His nostrils flared, and his eyes did that trick of glowing again—almost yellow instead of brown. He stepped even closer, gripping the sides of my robe at my chest. I caught his hands, unsure whether he was going to close or open it. I was unsure which action I wanted.

"Uh huh," he murmured in a smooth-as-whisky tone. "Real dick. Bigger than your dildo. Guaranteed to please." He lowered his head, and I found myself tilting my chin to let him brush his lips across mine.

For someone so fierce, he slid his mouth over mine slowly once. Again. Then his tongue swept between my lips, and my arms looped around his neck. With all of his pent-up energy, he was actually gentle.

Until he wasn't. He backed me against the wall beside the door and pinned my body with his, deepening the kiss until I forgot all about Jett Markle, or the job, or even what my name was supposed to be.

It was just him and me. His lips on mine. His large, hard body caging me in, the rock-solid bulge of his cock pressing into my belly. I could feel every hard, hot inch of him. Unlike Jett, Rob smelled good. Like hard work and hot man. I couldn't explain it, but it called to me. I craved it, wanted to breathe him in all the time. When he eased back, rubbing his lips like he was still tasting me, his lids were at half-mast.

"Think about my offer," he rumbled and released my robe. He set his hat back on his head. I had no idea how he'd done all that with his hat in one hand, but he had.

I drew in a shaky breath, my pussy clenching. "I will." The words wobbled as they came out.

Rob backed away, tipping his hat before he walked into the darkness.

As I pushed into the house, my legs trembled. And it wasn't from fear.

Damn.

Maybe I should've invited him in because the ache I'd felt for him before was nothing compared to this. One taste of Rob Wolf, and I was hooked. I was a DEA agent, but he was my drug. And I wanted more.

6

ROB

I WALKED BACK to Wolf Ranch with the taste of my mate on my tongue. I hadn't intended to go to her. After the pack meeting, I'd realized how fucking impossible this situation was and let my wolf lead.

I'd seen Markle's truck pulling away from her driveway, and my entire thought process changed. My wolf howled, knowing he'd been anywhere near our mate. Breathed in her scent, seeing her smile. Her scowl. Anything from her.

No matter the situation with my pack, this was personal. Markle might be a pain in the ass, but he wasn't getting Natalie. No. Fucking. Way.

I'd run the rest of the way to her place without even thinking.

I'd had a taste of her, and my wolf had been right. She was ours. I licked my lips then grinned. She tasted like strawberries and honey.

I'd just kissed my mate.

I chuffed a low laugh in the darkness. Yeah, my situation was as fucked as it could be with the pack demanding I mate a she-wolf and my true mate turning out to be the human next door, but that didn't stop the buoyancy in my chest at having been near her. Having kissed her. I felt like a middle school boy who'd had his first smooch or copped a quick feel.

My wolf wasn't happy I hadn't parted her robe, lifted her up so my dick was at her entrance and plunged into her, fucking her against the side of her house. My wolf wasn't happy I walked away at all. If it were the full moon, I wouldn't have been able to leave.

I might have lost control and done something regrettable because she wasn't a wolf and didn't know our ways. Didn't know it had been one deep breath, and I was done for. She was mine, forever. Somehow, I'd forced myself to leave her place tonight.

Humans didn't take kindly to being claimed before they knew a guy. At least that was what my brothers found, and I'd watched them fuck up. I didn't want to do the same. Oh, I'd fuck up. There was no help for it. The pack was going to lose their shit when they learned the truth, especially Nathan and anyone else who thought I was steering the pack wrong. It was the outcome, besides having Natalie for a mate, that was uncertain. I hadn't been alpha eighteen years to have it yanked for petty shit now. Who I mated wasn't petty, but the concept of it dividing the pack... that made me the only one to resolve it because I was the one who was causing the problem.

As I arrived back at the ranch house, I realized something was up. I paused, glanced at the place with all the lights on. No one should be there.

I jogged up to find Clint's parents' car parked in front, along with my brother Colton's. He and Marina were back from North Carolina. Funny how that brought a sense of relief, knowing I had both of my brothers home. Having my family back was huge.

It was as if this whole time—years—I'd been treading water, keeping the ranch going, leading the pack, doing everything expected of me except taking a mate, but none of it was for me. It was for them. For their future.

Now that they were back, I could breathe. Figure out my own future. I could think about myself and what my wolf wanted for five fucking minutes.

Although it didn't seem like that was going to start right now because something was fucking wrong, which meant my life was about to implode.

"There he is," Tom said from the front door, looking concerned. "You go for a run, son?" He glanced at my clothes because shifters didn't usually run in human form.

Tom moved to the side, and Colton came out onto the porch. "Heard about the meeting."

I growled. I really didn't want to fucking talk about the meeting. I wanted to thump my brother on the back and welcome him home.

Like everything else when it came to being alpha, I didn't get a break until the issue was put to bed. I said nothing, only nodded, and went past them into the house, heading straight to the kitchen. I paused in the doorway, took in the small group around the table. Clint, Levi, and the rest of the ranch hands sat with Janet and Boyd.

"What the hell are you all doing in my kitchen at midnight?" I demanded.

"Nathan Brown met with pack elders after the meeting," Janet said in a tight voice. "We weren't included, of course, because he knows our relationship with you, but the Thompkins told me. The elders are very concerned about your mating status and moon madness destroying the pack. Of course, they don't want to be absorbed into the Madison Range pack—it's not like they're getting into bed with them. At least not the way Ginny Thompkins portrayed it. But there's a lot of concern."

I slapped my palm down on the table. "I'm not going to succumb."

I hadn't meant to throw alpha power into my words, but it came out anyway, blasting everyone back in their seats, the coffee cups on the worn table rattling.

"I called a friend up in Manitoba," Tom said. His hair was more salt than pepper these days, but his calm demeanor and quiet way had been a good influence. I respected his words because he used them sparingly. "Their alpha's daughter hasn't been mated yet, and her father's dead set she only mate with an alpha. He wanted another Canadian, but it hasn't gelled. He'd like to arrange a meeting with you."

An arranged marriage?

No, my wolf snarled.

No fucking way. I kept my mouth shut, though. An alpha thought before he spoke. Even when it came to his mate.

"My brother should choose his mate," Colton said. I glanced over where he leaned against the back stairs, Marina tucked under his arm.

Tom nodded. "Of course, he should. But there's no harm in meeting the she-wolf, is there? It would show Nathan and the pack he's addressing their concerns."

I wanted to shout "No!" so the walls shook but bit it back. Stayed quiet. I wasn't Rob Wolf, the man. I was alpha, and that meant I had to listen to my pack, even about my fucking love life. It wasn't just my happiness and livelihood at stake here. If Nathan and the others tossed me out, everyone around me would have their life impacted and not for the better.

"I've arranged for her to visit," Tom said. "Just to give you a chance to meet her. If she's not the one, she's not the one. Just show the pack you're looking."

I wasn't looking. I'd found her. But I wasn't about to drop that bomb now, even if I did consider everyone in the room to be like family.

"Fine," I spat.

"What?" Boyd said, crossing his arms over his chest. "Fuck that."

He knew the truth about Natalie but kept quiet. I knew what he was saying, that Natalie should be claimed, be mine. Not some Canadian alpha's daughter. How was I going to be with Natalie again—because one taste was not enough—if a woman was coming to pack land just for me? I might not want her, but I wouldn't disrespect her feelings or intentions. She wasn't a pawn any more than I was.

I glanced at him, then Clint. "I'll meet her, and then I will decide." I was alpha. Tom was right. I had to show I was taking action for the pack. Even if the thought of receiving another female here killed me.

I said nothing more, only went up the backstairs and to my room.

Alone.

7

WILLOW

When I'd first arrived and chosen a bedroom, I couldn't pick the biggest, the one that Adam Shefield had used the fifty-plus years he'd lived in the house. His clothes still hung in the closet, his slippers tucked beneath the side of his bed.

Instead, I chose a smaller one down the hall, which turned out to be a good thing since it had rained overnight, and there was a small puddle on the floor in the big bedroom. It appeared the roof had a leak. I had to assume it was a new thing, but it would need to be fixed right away. Roof damage, especially bad enough to have water come all the way through a ceiling, could destroy a house.

A money pit, definitely.

I'd learned the guy had never married or had kids, which was why Natalie, being a great-niece, inherited. Also, because they had a musical connection. Adam had played fiddle, and Natalie became a concert violinist. I had to hope no one asked me where my violin was because I couldn't play a note to save my life.

My bedroom seemed to be for guests although I didn't know how many the old man had had. Natalie had visited when she was a kid but hadn't been back in years.

I'd emptied the few things from the closet—an old robe and a few moth-eaten sweaters on the top shelf. I'd vacuumed the rug, mopped the wood floor and even dusted. At least the room I was staying in was cleaned out. While I didn't want to mess too much with the real Natalie's inheritance, it also wouldn't look right if I didn't properly move in.

Downstairs, I'd thoroughly cleaned the kitchen and aired out the rooms.

After being closed up for months, the house was cleaner than the clothes I'd worn last night. I hadn't gotten dirty on my date. The only thing I could've done was dribble steak sauce on my shirt. But I'd wanted to shower the second he brought me home last night, the cloying scent of his cologne had lingered on my clothes... and still did in my room. I grabbed all my laundry and headed down to the cellar to get the washing machine running.

I'd always had a sensitive nose. Even now, I grimaced and held the stinky clothes away from my body. Growing up, my foster brothers used to purposely leave smelly things hidden in my room to drive me crazy.

I sighed as I lifted the lid on the washer and tried to figure out the buttons. The machine was avocado green and probably forty years old. I pushed the dial, and the water began to fill the basin.

I dropped the clothes in, then poured some soap in from the box on the shelf. I was used to the little pod things and had to hope I wouldn't suds the cellar. On my way up the stairs, I heard knocking.

I must be close to ovulation because my nipples hardened even before I had the conscious thought that it might be Rob, my cocky cowboy.

God, that kiss! A million—no a trillion—times better than Markle's. Markle's wasn't even a kiss in comparison. No, Rob Wolf had curled my toes last night, for sure.

The next time you come, it will be beneath me.

He was wrong. I'd come last night with the massaging showerhead thinking about him. And he was the guy I couldn't stop thinking about last night as I fingered myself to sleep again afterward.

But yes, I was definitely considering his offer. I'd been considering it non-stop since the moment he sauntered off into the darkness. And who walks in the dark, anyway? There was no moon last night at all, and the guy didn't have a flashlight.

He probably thought he could see in the dark. I remembered when I was a kid, I could. Until my foster brothers locked me in a dark closet to prove I was wrong. Then whatever superpower I thought I possessed drowned in a new fear of the dark.

The knock came again. When I opened the warped door, a dark-haired woman in her early thirties stood there with a smile and a plate of brownies in her hands.

"Hi." I pushed open the screen door.

"Hi! I'm Audrey Ames-Wolf, your new neighbor."

Wolf. I peered past her at the Wolf Ranch, as if that would clarify who this woman was. Hopefully she wasn't Rob's wife because that would make him a cheater, considering how he'd kissed me last night.

"I heard my brother-in-law barged in on you yesterday. I'm sorry about that. We didn't know you'd already arrived.

Rob's been looking in on the place. He was close with your uncle and felt responsible while you were away."

Brother-in-law. Good. "Yes, I met Rob." She didn't mention just *how* I met him, and I wasn't going to. "Come on in." I stepped back to invite her in.

"Here." She pushed the plate at me. "Brownies. I made them, but you can just throw them in the trash. My sister, Marina, is the baker in the family, and you'll meet her soon enough. She's… engaged to my husband's brother."

I stood there and stared at her trying to figure it out. "You married one Wolf, and your sister's engaged to another?"

She grinned. "That's right. But not Rob. He's not married. Single. *Very* single."

"Okay. Got it."

"Back to the brownies. They're a housewarming gift, but the gift may be that I tell you not to eat them. I'm a doctor, not a chef."

I led her toward the kitchen. "How about something to drink, and we won't eat the brownies?"

She laughed. "Sounds great. I hope Rob didn't make too bad of an impression. He seems gruff and grumpy, but he's actually a softie."

Softie?

Nope, it was plenty hard.

"Um, it wasn't so much gruff and grumpy…" My pussy clenched remembering the sight of his very long manhood straining his jeans. The sensation of it pressed against my belly. My mouth twisted into a wry smile. "It was more cocky."

"Oh!" Her laugh was musical. "I thought that was my husband's specialty. I guess all the Wolf boys have that in spades, though."

I shoved away my sudden interest in finding out everything there was to know about these Wolf boys. They hadn't come up in any part of my investigation, which meant they weren't involved with Markle. I liked the guys more just for that. I had Markle to worry about. That's why I was here, not to have a fling with a sexy rancher.

Oh God, I really wanted to have a fling with the sexy rancher!

I set the brownies down on the table. "I don't have much to offer you, yet, but I did buy some of these flavored seltzer cans. Are you a fan?"

"Sure," Audrey said.

I opened the fridge and stared at the cans. "Lemon or mandarin orange?"

"Mandarin, thanks." She took it and cracked it open while I opened a lemon one.

"So do you all live together there?"

She cocked her hip against the counter. "No. Boyd and I have a little cabin west of the ranch house, and I—we—also have a little house in town, which is easier when I'm on call or at the hospital late. I'm an Ob/Gyn."

"You live in both places?" I scrunched my forehead, trying to figure out how that worked.

"Just for now. We're newly married—still getting settled." Her hand drifted to her lower belly. The detective in me didn't miss the gesture.

"Oh, congratulations." I let my gaze drop to her belly, too.

"Oh!" She blushed. "Yes, I am expecting. It's not public yet. How did you guess?"

I liked Audrey already. She seemed open and friendly. No hidden agendas. A down-to-earth type. "You rested your hand there." I pointed. "Always a tell-tale sign."

"You have kids?" She looked around as if some were hiding behind the furniture.

"Me? No. Single."

"Your neighbor's interested in you," she replied with a grin, then took a sip of her drink.

I shrugged. "We had dinner. Nothing else."

She frowned, cocked her head to the side. She had sleek dark hair and wore glasses, but the way she studied me was more from keenness than confusion.

"He moves fast. I'm impressed."

I did, since I'd gone over and introduced myself, but I wasn't going to tell her that.

"Markle's a nice guy and all, but I don't see it getting all hot and heavy. I mean, he's got this... fake cowboy vibe about him. You know what I mean?"

"Jett Markle?" she asked.

I took a drink. "Yeah. Who did you think?"

"Rob."

I had butterflies in my stomach like a high school girl from just his name. "Rob?" I repeated.

"He's interested in you. And he won't be interested in knowing you went out with that jackass Markle." She pushed her glasses up her nose and set her drink on the laminate counter.

I already found that much out. What I needed to know was if Rob had anything concrete on Jett besides shooting his dog. "What's wrong with Jett?" I fished.

She pursed her lips as if she'd tasted something sour. "He's just a jerk. He's got a hard-on for your land."

"Did you just say hard-on?" I couldn't help but laugh, and she joined me.

"He does. I have no idea why, since you told him even before you got here you weren't interested in selling."

I shrugged. "I'm not. I am curious why he's so eager though. I mean... is there oil or something?"

"Who knows. But I was talking about Rob."

"Yes. Well, I've only spoken with Rob briefly." First in just a towel—with a vibrator in my pussy. And then in a robe—with his cock against my belly. So yeah. Just briefly.

"The Wolf boys know what they want when they see it, and Rob wants you."

I didn't doubt her since I'd seen the proof. All... nine inches of it inside his jeans.

"That's a little crazy." It was. The way he'd looked at me when he found me in the bedroom, the way he'd ensured the other person he was with didn't see me. The way he'd guaranteed me pleasure...

It was crazy, but that made me crazy, too, because I was still thinking about the possibility now. A fling would take the edge off, but I was supposed to be interested in Markle, not Rob Wolf. I'd be messing with my investigation.

No, my investigation was messing with my sexy times with a hot, bossy cowboy.

Her cell chimed, and she pulled it from her pocket. "Sorry." She read the screen. "Shoot. I've got to go. I'm on call, and a patient's water just broke."

"No problem."

"We should do a girl's night soon. Marina's just back in town, and I know she'd love to meet you."

"Sounds great." I led her back to the front door. It did, and it didn't.

I'd love to hang out with her, maybe get more information on Jett, but the more people I met and befriended under false pretenses, the more would feel betrayed when my real identity was revealed, and the real Natalie showed up. I wasn't here to make friends and have a good time. I wasn't here to fix up this old house although that was what I'd been doing all morning, and I still needed to get up on the roof.

"I'll be here working on the house."

She glanced around. "It's a nice place. Good bones. You could make it a bed and breakfast or something."

I shrugged. Even if it was up to me, I'd have no clue how to run a business like that. I didn't do hospitality. "Today I have to get up on the roof. There's a leak, and it's got to get fixed."

She went down the steps, then turned back, tilted her chin up to look at the front of the house. "Be careful up there. I don't want to see you in the ER."

8

ROB

I STAYED AWAY OVERNIGHT, my wolf keeping me awake. He was restless and riled after that kiss. After the pseudo-intervention in the kitchen. I'd just kissed my mate but was being pushed toward another woman. A she-wolf. Claiming and biting a female who wasn't your mate might or might not end the moon madness—the subject was up for debate. There were not scientific studies on wolf shifter physiology.

They were being thoughtful, in a matchmaker sort of way, but it might not actually solve my problem.

The only way to do so was to sink my teeth into Natalie's sweet flesh and permanently mark her as mine. The one my wolf wanted. If I claimed her, the moon madness would be gone for certain. But I'd be mated to a human.

I'd be dead from moon madness otherwise, meaning there would be a new alpha. Or, I'd be mated to a human and alive, but there would be a new alpha.

I didn't want to fuck my pack like that. So I was fucked.

I shifted my dick in my pants. I wasn't fucked. I *wanted* to be. By Natalie.

She was just down the road, no doubt getting off without me. Maybe even with Markle. She wouldn't dare go to him after the kiss we shared. That was *my* job now, to see to her pleasure. If she had needs, I'd meet them, whatever they were. Clint and Boyd had kept silent, understanding the situation I was now in. They had no answers.

I was damned if I did and damned if I didn't. Did the pack think I *wanted* to turn feral? To go so mad I couldn't shift back to human form? A danger to man and shifter alike? Wolves like that had to be put down before they injured someone.

That was why, after I'd had my third cup of coffee, that I might as well be damned. Again. I shouldn't have gone over there, confronted her about seeing Markle. Shouldn't have kissed her. I couldn't help it, just like I couldn't help it now. I didn't have to claim her. I could fuck her out of my system. Boyd and Colton had fucked their mates without biting them. If they could do it, I could. Hell, I wasn't a virgin. I'd fucked and not bitten a female before. But none of them had been my mate. I could do it. I'd rather die with a sated dick than with blue balls. I could let my wolf be happy for a little while before I had to give her up for the pack. For a Canadian she-wolf mail order bride.

My cell rang, and I sighed when I looked at the name of the caller. "What?" I barked at Boyd.

"Your mate's on her roof."

I pushed off the counter and stared out the kitchen window. "How the fuck do you know that?"

I couldn't see her house, so I grabbed my hat off the hook and stormed out the back door, the screen slapping behind me, so I could get a view of the Shefield house. I might have exceptional night vision, but I couldn't see a woman on the roof from this distance.

"Because Audrey went to visit her this morning, and Natalie told her she was going to fix a leaky roof."

"Why?" I stalked to my truck, my wolf panicking about our mate getting hurt.

"Because there's a fucking leak, and it rained last night," he repeated.

"No, why did Audrey visit?"

"Because it's neighborly. She took her brownies."

"Fuck neighborly. I thought you said your mate couldn't boil water. Is she trying to kill her?" I snarled, putting the truck into gear, the wheels kicking up dust with my haste to get down the road.

"Fine. I won't call next time your mate is in danger."

"You told your wife," I said, circling back to a big issue.

"Of course, I did."

"Did she tell Natalie she's my mate?"

"Of course not, you asshole. Natalie's new to town. If she's going to be your mate, then Audrey figured they should meet, since they'll be sisters-in-law and all."

"She's not my mate." I slowed the truck around the corner and went down the Shefield drive.

"Then why are you pulling up to her house? I know you're driving over there. If she wasn't yours, you wouldn't give a shit she was on the roof."

I turned off the engine, tore out of the truck when I saw my mate just where Boyd had said: kneeling two stories up on the fucking roof with a hammer in her hand.

"I don't know if I should thank you or punch you in the face for sticking your nose where it doesn't belong."

"I'm not the one you're angry at. If someone needs to be punished, it's your mate for putting herself in danger."

Well, fuck. That suggestion made me hard as stone. I'd like to punish her. Over my knee. I ended the call and shoved my cell back in my pocket. Boyd might have been right. The idea of taking that feisty redhead in hand was the best one I'd heard all day.

Just as soon as I got her down from the goddamn roof.

Crazy little human. What was she thinking? Did she not realize how fucking fragile she was? When her bones broke, they didn't repair overnight like mine. If she broke her neck, her life would end, just like that.

I wanted to shout up to her, but that would be foolish. Startling her while she was up there could be disastrous, even though she had to have heard me tear up her driveway. Instead, I checked out how she got up there. A ladder was on the roof of the wraparound porch, a window open right next to it, most likely her bedroom or the one next door. She either had no care for her safety or wanted to win the Darwin awards. The wooden ladder had to be older than I was and warped. It wasn't braced or anything on the roof. And that was just how she got up on to the main roof, not the fact that she was there to begin with.

I hopped onto the porch, then climbed onto the railing, turned and faced the house and reached up to grab the porch roof. With a hop, I pulled myself up, then swung a leg onto the shingles. With a little sweat and a whole hell of a lot of swearing, I pushed to my feet, then checked the stability of the ladder before using it to join her.

"What are you doing up here?" She knelt by a decent sized hole in the shingles. It hadn't been ripped off from the rain the night before, but maybe from the storms a few weeks ago, when one of our trees fell through the barn during Boyd's and Audrey's wedding reception.

"What the fuck are *you* doing up here?"

She waved the hammer she held in her left hand. "Fixing a leak."

"The only way to fix it is put on a new roof."

"Not happening." She was squatting down, and she shifted slightly to face me. At least she had on jeans and sturdy leather boots. I wouldn't have to punish her for wearing something stupid like flip flops. "I found a few shingles in the old barn. I'm giving it a patch for now."

"I'm not arguing with you about what you're doing, I'm arguing at the fact that *you* are doing it. It's dangerous as fuck up here. You could have slipped off, and no one would have known."

Her back stiffened, and her eyes narrowed. Her breathing picked up, and I couldn't miss the way her breasts rose and fell beneath her white tank top. Or the fact that her skin had a sheen of perspiration or that I could scent that tang of sweat along with her sweet essence. She had on more clothes than I'd ever seen her in, but she was still stunning. And now she was as pissed as me. It was obvious she didn't like to be told what to do. In a situation like this, thirty feet up? Too fucking bad.

"You're not my keeper," she practically growled, which made my wolf want to growl right back.

"It sure as fuck isn't Markle," I countered.

Her eyes narrowed, and her cheeks flushed. "It isn't you."

"It sure is, angel. Give me that hammer, and we'll get this patched. Then you're getting your hot little ass off this roof."

"I can patch it just fine, thank you." Her sass was supposed to piss me off. It only made me hard. Made me ache to sink balls deep inside her. But not up here on a fucking roof.

"You have two minutes to finish." I didn't move, just glared. Waited. My issue wasn't with her ability to fix the roof—she could do the job. Once she was down though, I was going to destroy that ladder so she couldn't get up here again.

She huffed, then slid one of the rectangular roofing sheets into place, hammered it along the top side. She did two more, covering the damaged area.

I held out my hand for the hammer. With a frown, she handed it to me.

"I'll go down first. You follow. Then we'll discuss your punishment."

Her mouth fell open, and one brow lifted, but I stood and went to the ladder. She hadn't moved.

"Punishment?"

I tipped my chin. "Bad girls get punished."

It was a loaded statement, especially given to someone who was far from submissive. I'd had women run scared... literally and figuratively, at my aggressive ways. With sex, I liked it rough. Wild. Lately, I'd avoided women because I felt almost... feral with the need to take. To dominate. To fuck hard and long. I didn't want Natalie to be afraid of me, but I needed to know how far she'd go with me. As my mate, I knew she wouldn't be all vanilla and missionary. I'd seen the damn dildo. But how far would she go?

"Are you serious?"

If there was a button on Natalie labeled *Fucking Pissed,* I just pushed it. Except her nipples popped through her tank top, telling me how much she loved the idea.

"Did you seriously get on the roof alone?" I countered. "One of the ranch hands does something like this, he'd be shoveling manure for a month. You'll only get your ass spanked."

She was still squatting down on the roof, but I couldn't miss the way she squirmed. "And you think you're the guy to do it?"

I tilted my head to the side, drinking in the sight of her. Feisty. Aroused. Pretending to be invincible. "Course, it's not punishment if you like it. We'll go with Plan B."

Her lips stretched into a grin. "Catch me if you can," she taunted and nimbly as could be, lunged for the ladder and swung a leg down onto it.

I cursed, throwing myself onto my belly to catch and hold the ladder for her, but she was already halfway down, grinning up at me with a wicked smile.

I climbed down as she went through the open window, then I picked up the ladder, chucked it off the roof where it landed on the ground with a loud crash.

"Watch out, angel. Your ass is now mine," I warned, laughter in my voice as I followed her into the house.

I was right. It was her room. Perfect.

So long as she didn't go for that pistol of hers.

But she didn't. She made it to the door, but I beat her, reaching past her head to slap my hand on it and slam it closed.

She spun about and was about to say something that would most likely get her in even more trouble, so I shoved her against the door and kissed her. This wasn't the tame kiss of the night before. No, this had all the pent-up energy since the first time I laid eyes on her right here. In just a towel and a dildo buried deep in her pussy. The next thing buried deep was going to be me.

She was hot and wild in my arms. Aggression, anger, need. Passion. It all came out of her into the kiss. Fuck, yes!

She gave as good as she got. She was a tiger, a wild one and was clearly in need of a good fuck.

I pulled back but held onto her biceps. "If getting your ass spanked gets you hot, then getting your ass fucked is a better punishment for a wild one like you."

She was aroused, our arguing blatant foreplay. The kiss... a match to the inferno between us. I was pushing it, pushing her. I had to know. For a woman with a passion and needs like hers, under-satisfying her was just as bad as pushing her too hard. I'd give her what she needed, I just had to find out exactly what it was.

An ass fucking? Yeah, that definitely jumped past first-base. But Natalie had been fucking herself with a huge dildo. No tiny vibrator for her. She knew what she wanted and went for it. I let her go and went around her bed to the nightstand. If a woman had a dildo, she'd have other toys, and they all had to be stored somewhere.

Just as I thought, when I opened the drawer, I found a small collection of toys.

"Bring it, cowboy," she challenged.

I laughed as I glanced from the drawer to her. "Let's see what you have in here for me to work with."

She watched me, lids drooping, pupils blown with need. She wasn't embarrassed, but I doubted anyone else knew the secrets the drawer said about her.

I reached in, pulled out a butt plug that was far from small and beginner in style as well as a small bottle of lube. My dick had never been harder. Pre-cum seeped from the tip and was no doubt marking my jeans.

"Yeah, you're definitely getting your ass fucked."

9

WILLOW

OH DAMN.

Hot, hot damn.

I'd never had a guy mess with me like this before. With Jett Markle, I was able to put up a wall or compartmentalize, especially since he was a suspected drug runner. Some kind of psycho-babble explanation for not letting a man in. Sure, it stemmed with the fucked-up childhood I had. Maybe I had daddy issues. Or maybe I never had any good example of love from the Carps. I'd had the opposite, using a rotating horde of foster kids not to support and care about but to line their pockets and get free labor on their ranch.

Later, when dating men, sex was okay, but not relationships. I never sought a connection. Never wanted one. Hell, never *felt* one. With anyone.

Until now. Until Rob Wolf and his dark gaze. His stern tone. His fucking protective streak a mile wide. Hell, everything about him pissed me off, made me giddy like a schoolgirl and made me horny as could be. Every thought of him made me hotter. That kiss the night before had been explosive, but his words now... holy fuck.

Spanking me? Fucking me in the ass?

Yes, please. I'd had anal sex before. I'd liked it, but I hadn't liked the guy I'd done it with all that much. I'd discovered I liked things dark. Kinky. A little wild. He'd gotten me off but hadn't lit my fire. But Rob?

It wasn't going to be punishment, and he knew it. The only way he'd truly punish me would be if he walked away like he had last night. Left me even needier than I was now.

That would be punishment for him, too.

Bring it, cowboy.

I suddenly realized that my whole adult life I'd been resistant, even bitchy to men, trying to find the one guy capable of taking charge of me—the hellcat.

It seemed I'd finally found him.

He pinned me with his dark gaze, holding the lube and my biggest plug between the fingers of one hand. "Clothes off, angel. It's time for your consequences."

This was the moment I went with it or walked away. Sure, it was my bedroom, but I knew deep down if I told him to slow his roll, he would. Somehow, he knew just how far to take this to make me hot. If anal wasn't my thing, I had no doubt he'd be up for something else.

I shook my head—not because I wasn't right there with him. Only because I wanted him to work harder for it. "Make me."

He grinned. "You like it rough, huh?"

I nodded, softening my knees, arms in front of me in a martial arts defense position.

Rob walked over with complete self-assurance and

tossed me over his shoulder. I'd twisted to dart away, but he was too fast. Too strong.

Maybe I didn't really want to get away. There was no maybe about it. I was right where I wanted to be and with exactly the right guy.

I laughed, kicking as he carried me to the bed, then flipped me onto my back and pinned my arms beside my head.

"Careful what you wish for, angel," he murmured.

Now that he loomed over me, it was even more clear how big he was. Not just his dick—all of him. I didn't find his size and strength threatening, though. Only arousing. The fact that he'd tried to protect me, not once but twice... felt good. I'd taken care of myself since... forever. It felt nice to have someone watching out for me, someone big and brawny enough to take on some of my burdens.

I hooked my legs around his waist and pulled hard, making him fall onto me.

He laughed again. "Careful, angel. I could crush a little thing like you."

I tightened my grip with my inner thighs. "I'm not that little."

He pulled his hips back—as if to show me how weak I was compared to him, then slammed them back in, the bulge of his cock grinding in the notch between my legs.

I moaned and rolled my hips to rub over his erection.

He tsked. "Not yet. Punishment before pleasure." He pulled back and flipped me to my belly, then tugged my wrists behind my back like I was under arrest. I hadn't experienced anything so hot in my life. I wondered if I should tell him about the handcuffs I had in my bag under the bed, but he leaned down to murmur in my ear, "Or at least *with* your pleasure."

And that was when my spanking began.

Oh my God.

He slapped my ass fast and hard, over my jeans as I wriggled beneath, giggling and trying to dodge his big heavy hand. Butterflies fluttered in my belly, my pussy grew slick and a fever took over my entire body.

It was exactly the perfect mixture of pleasure and pain. It stung, but the heat bloomed. It was the kind of thing you read about in trashy romance novels but didn't believe was really true. As the burn increased, I wanted more of it, even as I struggled to get free. It was a combination of being at his mercy, being punished for doing wrong, and yet he was touching me in a way that wasn't actually doing me harm. He knew exactly how this made me hot, how it turned him on, too, by having me to dominate.

He went on longer than I thought. I didn't know what I expected—a few swats, but he spanked me in earnest—maybe twenty-five times, then rolled me over on my back again and unbuttoned my jeans.

His dark gaze met mine. "That was for being up on the roof alone."

I toed my shoes off, letting them drop off the edge of the bed. He tugged my jeans and panties down my legs and onto the floor. "And this is for making me chase you." He took his hat from his head and dropped it on the floor beside him, then pushed my knees wide, dropped between my legs, and licked into me.

I gasped, knees clapping around his ears, shocked at the sudden delicious intrusion. This was *not punishment.* Oh, hell no.

"Uh uh," he warned, pushing my knees open butterfly style and sliding his palms under my ass. "You leave these knees wide or you're going to get a second spanking, and this time it will be my hand on your bare ass."

Oh God. This man.

I freaking loved the growled threats. Loved the way he licked my pussy like his life depended on it. Like he'd never tasted anything so sweet. I moaned as he nipped and sucked my labia, then found my clit with his lips and suctioned over it.

I screamed.

I might have slapped my knees closed again, but he forgot his threat because he was humming into my flesh as he sank his thumb into my pussy and massaged my anus with a finger slick with my arousal.

"Fuck," I moaned aloud this time. I'd never been so turned on in my life. I pressed his face into me, my inner thighs trembling, thighs flapping against his ears.

He lifted his head abruptly. "Don't come," he warned.

I lifted my head, looked down my body at him. His eyes were... golden but were filled with heat. His mouth and chin were slick with my blatant need.

"Wh-what?" Jesus, I had to come. I was so close.

He removed his thumb from my channel and delivered a light slap to my clit, making me startle, then clench. "You need me to spank your pussy?"

My cry echoed off the walls. I'd never met a dirty talker like him before, never knew it was so hot.

Rob picked up the butt plug and coated it generously with lube. And then, with no preamble at all, began to screw the thing into my ass.

I gasped, my anus squeezing tight in protest at the careful intrusion.

Rob played mock stern, catching my gaze. "Uh uh. Open

for it, angel. You were a bad girl. Now you're going to take it in the ass."

And just like that, I opened. Because apparently this man had now bought and owned my body with nothing but dirty talk and a skillful tongue. And hands. Hell, everything about this guy was skillful, and I hadn't even seen his dick yet.

I moaned as he eased the plug forward, stretching me wide, filling me. I whined as it went past the widest part and moaned with pleasure when it was finally seated. How could I not come? Every nerve ending in my body was firing hot.

The moment it was in place, Rob spanked my clit again. "You gonna keep them open for me, this time, angel?"

My brain was so scrambled, it was hard to figure out what he was asking, but I bobbed my head with enthusiastic agreement and set my feet on the bed as wide apart as they would go. Anything to make him continue. Make him deliver the orgasm that loomed so. Damn. Close.

I pressed my knees wide and waited, belly shuddering in with each breath, for him to lower his head again and show me how it was done.

After one dark and heated gaze meeting mine, he did. With gusto. Rob slid his tongue around the inside of my labia, then penetrated me with it, then flicked it over my clit. I panted, sweating, feverish. Ready to combust or die if I didn't come soon.

"Don't stop," I begged when he lifted his head. "Please."

"Aw, angel." His lips were even glossier with my juices now that the plug was in me. "I like it when you beg."

"Please." I was completely shameless. I wanted it so badly. "Don't make me get my gun."

He tossed his head back and laughed, and I paused to

stare at him. I'd yet to see him smile, and it transformed him from dark and broody to... relaxed. I had a feeling he wasn't like this very often, but then again, he was a man kneeling on the floor before a woman's pussy.

Rob slid two fingers inside me, holding my gaze once again as he swept them along my inner front wall. I was so tight with the plug and his fingers.

I cried out when he found my G-spot, and he curled his fingers over it. Once, then again.

"Now. Let me watch you come."

I'd never come on command before. I was able to climax fairly easily but never because someone told me to. Sex with Rob wasn't going to be anything like I'd ever experienced. And with that one word, *now,* I came, my inner walls clenching around his fingers as I squeezed and released the plug. The combination of attention to both my holes had me coming harder than I'd ever known.

I screamed and nothing like the day before when he'd walked in on me. This was as if he'd taken over my body, and it was his to command, to rule. Time ceased to exist, only the way he wrung pleasure from my body. I finally lay there, replete and sated, wilted and sweating.

"We're far from done, angel."

The clank of a belt buckle followed by the slide of a zipper had me opening my eyes. I lay there and looked as Rob opened his pants. He was watching me in return. I still wore my tank top and bra, but I was splayed lewdly on the bed, the wide base of the butt plug parting my ass cheeks.

He leaned down, took off his boots, then stood back up. From my position, he was so tall, so imposing. The scent of my arousal was in the warm air. Only a soft breeze from the open window stirred the air. All was quiet except for my ragged breathing and the pounding of my heart.

His hands went to the top of his jeans and my gaze lowered.

"Want to watch?" he asked.

I nodded, licked my lips.

His hands moved upward to his plaid shirt, and he tugged it open, the snaps giving way.

I stared at the smattering of dark hair on his chest that tapered to chiseled abs and then into a line that disappeared behind the open zipper as he dropped the shirt at his feet.

Holy hell, he ate his vegetables as a kid. Broad shoulders, tanned skin, chest hair—I liked a little hair on a guy. Gyms should have a barn room for cowboy exercises like tossing hay bales and wrangling cows because Rob was rock hard... everywhere. I couldn't miss the thick bulge in his jeans, and I watched as every inch of it was revealed as he pushed the denim down over his narrow hips. He took his pants and boxers off, but I wasn't paying that any attention. I was staring, wide eyed, opened mouthed, at his dick.

It was bigger than my dildo. Thicker. Longer. The taut skin was darker than on the rest of his body, smooth as if so engorged, it couldn't get any bigger. The crown was blunt and huge, and I knew it was going to rub over all kinds of delicious places inside me. My pussy clenched in anticipation, but that wasn't where he intended to put it.

I'd never thought this before, but... was he going to fit?

No wonder it went down the inside of his jeans.

He gripped the base, stroked it once, then again.

"Take off your shirt, angel. Let me see all of you before I flip you over and get in your ass."

I pushed up to sitting and lifted my tank over my head, then shucked my bra as he continued to work himself.

He groaned when he saw my breasts. They weren't big. Or small. I kind of liked them, with their little pink tips.

From the way Rob's jaw clenched and pre-cum seeped from his dick, he did too.

"Fuck, there's so much I want to do to you."

In the blink of an eye, he grabbed one ankle and rolled me onto my belly.

"Grab a pillow and put it under your hips. You're going to need it."

I did what he said as he grabbed the lube again and worked it all the way down his length, so he was liberally covered. His clean hand came down on my left butt cheek with a crack. "Ass up. Head down, angel. Oh, look at you. You can be a good girl sometimes, can't you?"

The one orgasm had relaxed me, made me hot and ready for more, but his talk riled me up.

I lay over the pillow and looked back at Rob standing at the side of the bed, like a big, dark haired Viking who was planning on marauding my ass.

"You're fucking gorgeous." He stepped closer, reached down and carefully pulled the plug from my ass. I gasped at the action then again when one of his slick fingers circled me there, then slid in. "Ready, angel? You're going to love your punishment. And so am I."

10

ROB

MY WOLF WAS PUSHING me to lay my body over hers, to feel every inch of her silky skin against mine, to slide deep into her pussy and fuck her, knowing how wet and receptive she was.

Then sink my incisors into her shoulder. They'd dropped when she shifted her hips up in the air, showing off her plugged ass and pink pussy. I'd fuck her there, but later. First, I was giving her what we both wanted.

It was the perfect sign of domination. The most intimate of connections. The most powerful of trusts. Her ultimate submission. The fact that someone as strong and self-sufficient as Natalie would be sprawled over her bed, parting her knees even wider as I watched, openly giving herself to me to claim her ass, blew my mind.

When she wiggled her hips, I carefully pulled from her the plug she'd taken so beautifully. Dropped it on the bed.

My hand was covered in lube from coating my dick, and I wanted to ensure she was as slick as possible. I was big. It was clear she'd done this before—she wasn't nervous or tense, only eager—and I tried to push that thought away or I'd have to go hunt the guy down and kill him. But he'd just been practice for her. Still, I assumed I was bigger based on the way she'd stared, almost bug eyed, when I took my jeans off.

I wouldn't hurt her. Sure, I'd spank her ass, definitely fuck it. But I'd never, ever hurt her. So when I easily slipped one finger into her tight back entrance without any negative response from Natalie, I added a second. Only then did she moan and push back, taking the two digits even deeper. I added a third and dripped more lube from the bottle over them, working it in. When I held my fingers still, she thrust back, lightly fucking herself on them. That was when I knew. It was time.

I grabbed her tank top and slid my fingers free, using it to wipe the excess lube off. With one hand, I aligned my dick up at her prepared hole and pressed then grabbed her hips.

I was careful. Slow. I took my time to let her relax, and I watched as she finally began to flower open, wider and wider. She moaned into the bedding as the head of my dick stretched her open. All at once, with the lube aiding the way, I popped past that tight ring of muscle and got inside her. She clenched around me as I held myself still, let her adjust.

Her fingers clenched the quilt as she groaned, low and deep at my entry. Her pussy was dripping, her arousal shiny and slick down the inside of her thighs. When I reached around her hips, I found her clit all hard and swollen. Her body was responsive, awakening her need to be taken like this.

"Bad girls get a dick in their ass, but good girls get it deep and get to come."

She moaned.

I dropped one hand on the bed by her hip as I began to slowly work my way into her. Back and forth, a little more of my dick each time. Shit, it felt so good. Tight. Hot as hell.

"Ever had anything like this in you before, angel?" I breathed. Sweat dotted my brow at my restraint.

She shook her head, her red hair a wild tangle about her face. Her eyes were closed, her mouth parted.

"Do you want me to tell you what I see? I see a gorgeous woman all feisty and wild, tamed by a big dick. Don't worry, I won't give away your secret, that you like me to take control, that you'll lift your ass and give it to me."

"Rob," she begged. I wasn't sure if she wanted even more or if she liked it when I said filthy things.

"Only me, Natalie. I'm the only one who will see you like this. The only one whose dick will bottom out in this tight hole. The only one who will ever hear you scream your pleasure as you milk the cum from my balls."

"Oh my God," she moaned. "I'm going to come from you talking."

I grinned. Fuck, that alone felt good. The feel of her so tight and hot practically strangling my dick was going to finish me too soon. I'd just given her all of my inches, and my balls were pulled up tight. I felt the need to come build at the base of my spine.

I began to move then, pulling back so that only the flared head was caught inside her, then filled her all the way a second time. She began to move then, to shift her hips in a motion that made her need grow. I loved her wantonness. I watched her carefully, adjusting my pace to how she liked it, to the way she moaned, begged, pushed back.

Words came from her lips, but they were lost on me. All breathy and full of need. I knew how she felt. I wasn't going to last much longer. I reached around again and found her clit, all distended and hard. Flicked it once.

She clenched down on me and moaned. I flicked it again, this time harder, and she screamed, "Yes!"

When I pushed into her all the way for the last time and came, I pinched her clit, setting her off. As I shot my cum into her hot ass, she clenched down, ensuring she took all of it deep into her.

Sweat bloomed across her skin, her moans and sounds of pleasure filled the air. I couldn't do anything but absorb the heat of her. I saw my mate lost in her own epic orgasm. I breathed in the musky scent of our fucking, untamed and wild. I wanted to taste the sweat on her skin, but I didn't dare get my mouth near her. Not now, not when I was in the throes of the best orgasm of my life.

It couldn't get better than this. Well, it could. It would when I officially claimed her. I had to wonder, if I felt like I was going blind by coming in her ass, I'd surely die of pleasure when I sank my teeth into her and marked her forever as mine.

11

WILLOW

"UM, WOW."

After how dominant Rob was in bed—and out, I wouldn't have taken him for a cuddler. But there I was, wrapped up in his arms, the soft fur of his chest tickling my back. He'd brought a washcloth to clean me up, and he now lay behind me, his muscled arm draped over my waist, his hand cupping my breast.

"Tell me about yourself, Natalie Shefield." Idly, his thumb played with my nipple which was quite distracting. Even after everything we'd just done—and my bottom was a little sore—his touch was arousing.

I winced at the name. *Natalie Shefield.* It sounded so wrong on his lips. I wasn't the sappy type, but damn if I didn't want to hear my real name in his deep rumble right now, especially after what we did. There didn't need to be affection or commitment tied to sex. Hell, I was the queen of that country. With Rob, it felt different. The connection was intense, almost visceral and perhaps that was why it felt so guilty. That while I gave myself to him so completely just a few minutes ago with my body, I could only lie to him with my words now.

There couldn't be any truth in my words, that the *real* me had to remain a secret. Not only outright lying but lying by omission too.

I rolled in his arms to face him. Up close, I could see his dark beard coming in. He was the kind of guy who had to shave every day. I wondered if he ever grew a beard, maybe in the winter and what he'd look like. Hell, what it would feel brushing over my thighs.

He was watching me, patient and quiet. What could I say? I searched my mind for something true. "I like Greek salad and gyros," I blurted, thinking of the gyro place by my apartment in Phoenix.

He grinned. "That might be tough in Cooper Valley, but I'll look into it."

I smiled back, suddenly floating. He wanted to find me a gyro shop? Who was this guy? We just had the randiest sex ever, and now he was acting like Prince Charming, post orgasm? That never happened. Usually it was pants on and out the door—for both of us. I mean, usually if a guy stayed, I was shoving him out the door. I didn't do sleepovers or morning afters.

This one wanted to find me gyros. And I seemed to like it.

"What's your plan here? You sticking around? You told Boyd you didn't want to sell the place."

Aw, fuck. I really wanted to keep this about the real me, but it seemed that would be impossible. I drew a breath. I had no idea what the real Natalie's plans were. I'd spoken with her before I arrived, knew she was getting a Master's degree in music theory—where I couldn't even hold a tune in the shower—and probably settling here in Montana because she was barely getting by as a musician in the big city. While she may have thought a mortgage-free ranch would be cheap, the bad roof was an example of the way this place might bleed her dry.

"Yeah, I don't know yet. I'm kind of figuring things out as I go."

Not a lie.

"Are you going to look for a job? Or... try to ranch?" he asked doubtfully.

I pushed up on an elbow, puffing my chest up. "What, you don't think I could ranch?"

He dropped to his back, hands up like he was surrendering. "I didn't say that. I'm quite sure you could do quite a few things on your own that most single women couldn't. Handle a weapon, for one. You gonna tell me what that's about?" He glanced over my shoulder at the nightstand where my gun had been the day before.

"It's downstairs on the kitchen table."

He frowned.

"I was on the roof, remember?"

I noted the look of concern on his face again. Like he thought I was on the run or someone was after me. Why I needed to move a gun around the house with me. I should be thankful for him not being the kind of guy who worried a little-ole-thing-like-me might shoot herself. He wasn't questioning my abilities, just the need for it.

It was damn sweet of him, his protectiveness, even though he was way off the mark.

"No one's after me," I said.

Huh. I also noted his eyes were darker than I thought. I

could've sworn they were golden before. And I'm pretty good at remembering faces. It was part of the training.

"What color would you say your eyes are?" I asked, not only curious but eager to change the subject.

He stared back at me, his expression suddenly blank. After a beat too long, he said, "Well, that was an obvious redirect." Yeah, he'd caught on. "You think I'm dumb enough to fall for that?"

Why did I feel like his words were also a redirect of his own? I narrowed my eyes at him.

He arched a brow at me.

"I like to be prepared." I swallowed. What could I say that wasn't a lie? That would show him the real me? I wanted to offer that right now. I had the urge to give him something I never gave out—not even when I wasn't undercover. "I grew up in foster care," I admitted.

He went still, even his breathing slowed.

"I was sort of... scared a lot growing up."

A rumble came from his chest.

"Nothing terrible," I added quickly when his face suddenly turned stormy. "Just not safe."

This man had the protector vibe in spades.

I sighed, rolled onto my back and stared up at the way the sunlight cut a triangular shape across the ceiling. "I had a rotating stream of foster siblings from terrible backgrounds and... other stuff. The family I was with last, they earned money from the state off of us kids. Anyway, one of the first things I learned to do when I left was shoot a gun. I needed to know I could look after myself." I turned my head, looked at him. "You know?"

"What about your great uncle? Shefield wouldn't take you in?"

I froze. Oh God! What had I said? I wasn't Willow Johnson, the orphan. I was supposed to be Natalie Shefield. I had to think fast. "It was just a few years," I said quickly. "While my mom was going through some stuff. She didn't want the rest of the family to know I'd been taken away from her."

Oh. My. God. I really fucked up.

I guess it showed how much this man had gotten under my skin. How much I wanted to show him the real me.

Rob seemed to absorb the information without any doubt, which made me feel even worse about deceiving him.

He blinked at me. "Have you had to use the gun?"

"No." I let out a forced laugh. The lie tasted like ash in my mouth. "But I keep it close. You know, for when strangers barge in on me masturbating."

That distraction worked. His eyes crinkled and lips curved up. He studied my face like he wanted to memorize it. "I'm sorry about your childhood."

I was unprepared for the sharp blast of emotion that followed his words.

I never allowed myself pity, but it seemed some of it had been bottled up all these years because tears suddenly popped into my eyes. I instantly rolled away from him to hide them, but he caught my arm and turned me back.

"It's okay," he said softly. "We all have wounds."

"Yeah?" My voice wobbled. "How about you, cowboy? What are your wounds?"

I didn't expect him to answer. He'd been nothing but cocky and self-assured with me. No hint of vulnerability for miles. But he stared into my eyes. "I took over running the ranch and raising my brothers when I was sixteen. It wasn't so bad—we made it through. But I never got to choose my life. My future got decided for me the day my parents died in a car crash."

I reached out to run my clipped fingernails over the soft

curls of his chest hair. "Your future's still in front of you," I reminded him softly.

His gaze traced my face. He reached out and ran the backs of his fingers across my cheek. "Yeah. It is."

A shiver ran down my spine although I couldn't identify its source. It wasn't a warning—although I got that kind of prickle sometimes. It wasn't sexual. It was more like... recognition. It scared the hell out of me. I pulled away, and he let his hand drop, as I pushed up to sit.

"Well," he said lightly, climbing out of the bed, "if you want to target practice, we have a makeshift range on my property." He picked his boxer briefs up from the floor and pulled them on, which was a shame. Rob, naked, was a sight.

I was here on a job not to date the cowboy next door. But target practice was part of the job, wasn't it? So was finding out what Rob knew about Markle although that excuse was flimsy, and I knew it. From what he'd made clear the night before, Rob held no positive feelings for the guy long before I arrived. That meant they had some kind of beef between them. I doubted Rob knew his neighbor was a drug runner. Knowing how black and white Rob was, he'd have turned him into the law. He knew something about Markle, and I wanted to know what it was.

"I'd love that." I climbed off the other side of the bed and went hunting for my clothes.

"Great." He zipped up his jeans then grabbed his shirt off the floor. "Tomorrow? One o'clock?"

Little bubbles of excitement fizzed, even though I was telling myself this was for work. *Work.* "I'd love that. I'll see you then."

He grinned, then looked down to do the snaps, covering up his gorgeous chest. Sex definitely put a smile on this guy's face. He was not the grouchy grumpy guy Audrey had described. Not at all, at least not now. Of course, he'd just come in my ass, so I had a feeling I was going to beat anyone in a making-Rob-smile competition.

He pointed at me. "Stay off your roof. You take a risk like that again, you won't sit down for a week because you won't get the fun kind of spanking. I'm serious, Natalie."

The threat was high-handed and ridiculous, but the sexual charge between us made it totally sexy. I suddenly found myself wanting to defy him, just to get the promised punishment, although the good kind.

"I can take care of myself." I fastened my bra and went to grab a new shirt from the dresser.

He finished putting on his boots. "I know that, angel. But you're not invincible, and you don't have to do it all on your own."

That wasn't true—I did. Or was that just what I preferred? It was hard to tell. Still, the idea of letting this big fierce cowboy think he was taking care of me had a strong appeal.

Too bad I wasn't the real Natalie Shefield, here to stay. Once Markle was behind bars, I'd be back to my desk in Phoenix. Back to a new bad guy... which was definitely job security. Neither the bad guy or my desk in the desert sounded all that appealing right about now. Living on a ranch with a sexy neighbor seemed so much better.

Too bad there was zero chance for us because there was a *real* Natalie Shefield waiting to move to the house she'd inherited. I actually liked this guy beyond what he could do in bed, and it should have made me feel amazing, but it just... sucked.

12

WILLOW

I HEARD the clank of metal hitting metal as I crept through the dark and a blast of satisfaction ran through me. My instincts had been right to come out here at night. They never failed me.

Night goggles in place to help me see in the moonless sky—thanks to the DEAs fancy supply closet—I moved forward in a crouch, dressed in black with black smudges on my face to mute the glow of my pale skin. I had my Glock with me this time. And a large hunting knife. And an infrared camera to get evidence.

Markle was moving something.

At night.

In the dark.

And somehow, I seriously doubted it was just cattle although that was what I was seeing through the goggles being loaded into a truck.

This was my favorite part of the job—the solo surveillance work. I liked it far better than using my femininity to milk a guy for information. Or boring desk research. I enjoyed the risk of it. The skill and physical prowess required to stay quiet, blend in. While I'd never hunted animals, there was definitely a hunter in me. Stalking my prey out here in the dark, while breathing the cool mountain air, made me feel alive.

I slipped forward, through the fence and onto Markle's property. I stayed low, near the telephone line. There wasn't much to hide behind, but I could always drop to my belly in the tall grass if I needed to.

There. I heard the clank again and the soft low of a cow. When I got close enough to see better, I crouched and took out the camera, adjusting the telescope lens to use it like binoculars.

It was a cattle trailer, and indeed, the cattle were in the chute ready to be loaded, but Markle was loading a few crates into the back. I snapped a dozen photos, switched to the non-infrared setting and clicked some more. My pulse raced. I had to get down there and find out what was in those crates. I crouch-ran forward, squatted, took some more photos.

A man started loading the cattle. By the time I got close enough, he'd shut the back gate on the trailer and climbed in the driver's seat. The engine of the truck rumbled to life and pulled away from the cattle chute and down the dirt drive.

Shit!

I took a risk and darted forward faster, as if I might miraculously catch sight of something else before it left. It was a typical livestock hauler. An eighteen wheeler with a metal slatted cargo area that I guessed by weight, not number of animals. I guessed Markle had loaded about five cows after I put on my goggles, the cover he needed to keep from being looked at too closely.

Realizing it was pointless to follow, I squatted again and took pictures of it leaving, getting a close up of the plate, the driver and each open window of the trailer.

He had to be moving drugs. Why else would he load up at night? Sure, it was hot, but I lived in Phoenix. *That* was hot.

I'd just expected more—a larger shipment, multiple trucks. Something obvious.

Maybe this was part of the genius of the operation—just one cow trailer at a time across the border to Canada. Nothing big enough to raise suspicion. I'd have to call my boss to have the plate checked at the border, to confirm that was the true destination. It wouldn't be stopped. We needed to arrest the source, not the specific driver.

I'd have to come back every night to see how often this happened. Fortunately, I hadn't had to kick Rob out of my bed to come here tonight. That would've been hard to explain away. He'd been pissed I'd gone out with Markle. I could only imagine what he'd do if he found out anything else.

I needed to figure this out. It was my job, and that was why I was here.

I wanted to get inside that barn and other outbuildings to search for drugs or evidence of drugs. But that was highly risky, and if Rob got a whiff of it, not only would he learn the truth, but he'd be pissed as hell. I sighed, realized I was thinking about the hot neighbor too much, worried about his reaction to my job and the case. My body heated at what I'd done earlier with him. I clenched my bottom, remembering how big he'd been, how he'd actually fit. That was why I was sore, even now hours later.

But I had to focus on my reason for being in Cooper Valley. I'd seen the cases, the animal hauler. I knew how they were leaving, but how were they arriving at Markle's property? The same way? Were the cows grazing his pasture rotating cattle, brought in to hide the incoming drugs and shipped out to do the same?

I didn't want to blow my cover by pushing things. I'd only had one date with Markle, and if I moved too fast, I'd end up in his bed or possibly dead. I wasn't sure which was worse. I had to have patience until I had real evidence that could be used against Markle and Murrieta. To put them away for life.

I lay down in the long prairie grass to see if anything else happened, but it went dark and quiet. With my goggles, I watched a few of the guys head in the direction of the barn where I assumed there was some kind of bunk house. Markle headed to his fancy ranch house. I took off the goggles and watched lights go on and off in the house, following his path to bed. After an hour of waiting, the light in—I assumed—his bedroom went out. I gave up the watch and went back to report to Vaughn.

He'd appreciate the photos, but that wasn't enough to bring in a team to make an arrest. I'd need more evidence than that to crack this case. When I did, I'd see Markle and Murrieta behind bars. I'd get that promotion and a new case, far from Cooper Valley, Montana. Two days ago, that was what I wanted. Now? I had no idea why I was questioning the plan.

Yeah, I did. It was a brawny cowboy with a big dick who'd proved he knew how to use it.

13

ROB

GROWING UP, having a wolf inside me had never been an issue. It was like having a weird friend always with you, whether it was to get you in trouble or to pull you from it. For me and Boyd and Colton, even Clint, too, it had been both. We'd also helped each other along with the good and the bad. Then we'd learned how to shift, to let our wolves out. To run.

Then our wolves had started to prod us toward finding our mate, letting it be known as a sadness, a frustration, a *need.* I knew how that felt. I probably had the crankiest wolf out of the four of us. Clint was now in second place. As for Boyd and Colton, they'd found their mates, and their wolves were calm. Happy. Settled. Hell, sated.

I tested the water in the shower, then stepped under the spray. I was sated. What guy wouldn't be after what Natalie and I did the day before. I'd found my mate. My wolf had scented her and let it be known no one else would do. Then I'd gotten her beneath me. Naked. I'd gotten in her as she submitted. The only thing I hadn't done was bite her.

After coming harder and more powerfully than I ever had in my life... and in her snug little ass no less, I should have been in bliss. Oh, I had the loose gait of a well fucked man. I also had the grin of a guy who'd dominated the hell out of a woman and satisfied her in a dark, feral way she didn't even know she craved.

But I hadn't bitten her.

That alone had my balls aching. My heart longing to separate the distance between us. My dick thick and hard between my thighs. I was sated of cum, but there was more. An endless supply for my mate, and I wanted to put it all in her.

I gripped my dick at the base, stroked it from root to tip, working it as I'd want Natalie to do. I thought of her mouth and how much of it she'd be able to fit into her throat. It wouldn't be all of it, but the base, filthy side of me wanted to see just how much, to watch her eyes widen knowing she'd never get it all before she choked.

Slapping my hand against the wall, I let my head drop as I got myself off. It didn't take long. Not last night before I went to bed. Not this time, less than an hour before she was to show up. As my cum spurted onto the tiles in long thick ropes, I knew my wolf was in charge. He'd stay that way until I dealt with my shit and made Natalie Shefield mine. I just had to figure out how to do that. Because while Boyd and Colton had given in to their wolves, I might not be able to give in to mine. I was alpha, and the pack came first, even over a mate.

An hour later, Natalie was at the door, and my wolf practically licked his chops in glee. Happy to see her, eager to fuck her. I didn't blame the animal within. I felt the exact same way.

I kissed her because I wanted to. I kissed her because I needed to. I kissed her to let her know she was mine without words. And because I couldn't wait another fucking second to do so. She tasted as I remembered. Spicy. Hot. And the kiss? Wild and a little uncontrolled, as if she craved as much as I did.

Her hand knocked off my hat. Mine found her breast over her t-shirt. My leg settled between hers, and if she rode my thigh a little, I didn't fucking mind.

I lifted my head, took a deep breath. "Fuck, woman."

"I was just thinking that," she replied, kissing along my jaw.

"If I get you in my bed, you're not getting out today. You've got two other holes I've yet to play with."

She groaned, and I could have sworn it was more growl than anything else.

"Besides, if you're here to target shoot, that means you're armed." I stepped back. "I don't mess with an armed woman."

Her fiery hair was pulled back in a low ponytail. She wore no makeup, but the flush I brought to her cheeks made her stunning. In jeans, boots and a white t-shirt that was modest yet sexy as hell. She was low maintenance, and while there was no doubt she was all woman, she wasn't girly like Audrey or Marina.

"Maybe I should pull it out, get you to do what I want."

I couldn't help but laugh. "Maybe I'd have stage fright."

Her gaze raked down my body in a slow perusal, and there was no way she could miss my hard-on. "Not a chance."

I grinned then led her out the front door. "Come on, we shoot behind the barn."

"How about a wager?" she asked.

I stopped and faced her, waited for her to continue.

"A sex wager."

I smirked, amused by her as much as aroused. "Sounds good to me."

"A shootout. Winner picks the kind of sex."

My dick punched against my jeans. "What if there's something I don't want to do?"

She arched a red brow and stared. "I highly doubt there's anything you won't do."

She was right. Except... "I don't share." The three words were deep and sharp.

Her smile slipped, and she nodded. "Sounds good to me."

We made it the rest of the way to the far side of the barn in silence. The construction work on the barn was almost complete. Before she left for North Carolina with Colton, Marina had offered suggestions to the trusses, so they were reinforced for superior durability. The supports were in and so was the sub-surface of the roof. The new shingles had to go on, which prompted me to add Natalie's roof to the contractor's tasks.

The back doors were open, and I'd set a few weapons down on a table.

"I assume you'll use your Glock?" I asked as she pulled the weapon from the back of her jeans.

"A rifle's a good choice around here," she said, running her hand over it, then lifting it up, checking to see if it was loaded with an easy skill of someone who's used one before and often. "Got a lot of wild animals?"

"Bears up in the hills although I like to give them room, so I don't have to shoot them."

She smiled. "That works. Jett Markle said he saw wolves."

I stilled but grabbed a box of bullets to keep from wanting to go over to Markle's land and shoot the fucker.

"You know how I feel about the guy. Let's not ruin our afternoon talking about him. I assume your Glock is loaded?"

"Of course."

I grabbed the rifle and two boxes of bullets, one for her Glock and one for my gun. This was Montana. We had many weapons and were prepared to use them all.

"The target's over there. I put the first paper sheets out earlier. Grab the hearing protection?" I tipped my head toward a stack of hay bales in the distance and Natalie grabbed the ear plugs. Beyond it was nothing but open pasture for miles and was wide open on both sides. If someone happened into view, we'd know well before they got in the line of fire.

I led her to where we stood to shoot, two hay bales stacked to rest bullets and unloaded guns. I left the extra target papers there earlier.

"Warmup round?" she asked, watching as I loaded the rifle.

I clicked it shut and aimed the barrel at the ground. "All right. Ladies first."

She put her ear protection in, moved a few steps away, and stood so her right leg was forward and raised her arm. Looking my way, she waited for me to get my ear plugs in, then focused on the target. Fired.

I had no idea if she was hitting the target. My gaze was on her. The way she stood, confident in her shooting. The vibe of power she was giving off was hot as hell. It might have also been the way she filled out her jeans or the curve of her breasts beneath the snug t-shirt. Or the red hair that caught the sunlight.

Fuck, she was incredible.

When her cartridge was empty, she aimed her gun at the ground and slid it open. I took her place and looked at the targets. All of her shots were neatly placed around the bulls-eye. She handled a weapon like Colton did, with military precision. She hadn't mentioned she'd been in the service, and I had to wonder the story she wasn't telling me. She'd said she'd been scared. While the idea of her being afraid of someone didn't sit well with me, I was reassured by her skills. No guy was going to get past her bullets. Not with her aim.

I lifted the rifle, aimed. Fired.

"Not bad." She set her empty weapon on the hay bale. I did the same, and we walked in companionable silence with new target sheets across the field.

When we returned, she loaded her Glock. "How's the shootout going to go?"

I shrugged, looked from her to the prepared targets.

"Fifteen shots. Closest to center wins."

"Sounds good."

We reloaded.

"I'm guessing ladies first again?"

I only grinned at her in reply.

She took her position again.

"Angel," I called.

Looking over her shoulder at me, she quirked a brow.

"Use your left hand."

Her mouth fell open. "How... I... what...?"

"You're left handed. I assume that's your dominant hand, yet you did your warmup round with your right."

She looked more surprised now than she did when I'd caught her masturbating.

"You like it when I call the shots in bed, angel? Is that why you're shooting with your weaker hand, so I can win?"

She pursed her lips and her eyes flecked with fire. Oh yeah, there was my girl. She switched her stance, raised her arm and barely glanced at the target. Fired.

That was what I thought.

I walked up to her, got so close my chest bumped into her breasts. "You hold back like that on me again, you'll get my belt on that pretty ass of yours. I want all of you, angel."

I took my shots, but I knew the outcome. I could shoot someone, but I wasn't trained in it more than practicing here on the ranch. I was alpha. I led.

We walked to the targets. She'd blown a hole through dead center, not a bit of paper separated one shot from the next. Unlike my target. I was close to center, but the winner was obvious. There was much more to Natalie Shefield than I ever imagined. I was going to spend my lifetime learning all her secrets. Every. Single. One.

"Well, angel. How do you want me? On top? You want to ride my dick? How about I lick your pussy until you come a few times, then you decide?"

She slid her palms over my chest and glanced up at me through those cinnamon lashes. "How about...we wash the sweat off in the shower, you lick my pussy until I come a few times, and then I decide?"

My mouth watered at the thought of tasting her. Getting her scent all over my face. "It's wrong to throw you over my shoulder when you won, isn't it?"

She flicked those eyelashes at me. "It is when we're both holding weapons, big guy."

Taking the rifle out of my hands, she settled it on her shoulder, just like a trained soldier.

Huh. There was definitely something she wasn't telling me. She'd been in the military or had some kind of training. This wasn't just a girl who took herself to a shooting range on weekends because it made her feel safe. I'd bet she'd even win in a shootout against Colton.

It bothered me that I didn't know her full story, but I definitely would. I intended to find everything out about Natalie Shefield I could. Starting with how she sounded screaming in the shower.

I put the rifle away in the barn and *then* I tossed her over my shoulder because I knew my mate liked to be conquered and also because I couldn't wait to touch her any longer.

Luckily, Colton and Marina were in Cooper Valley, so I didn't have to kick them out of the house. Because I definitely would have. I was going to make my mate scream, and I didn't want anything inhibiting her. I hadn't been joking when I told her I didn't share.

I kicked the front door shut behind us then carried her upstairs to the master bedroom and directly into the bathroom I'd remodeled myself.

She started stripping the moment I put her feet down, and I had to suppress the growl that came rocketing up my throat at every inch of bare skin she exposed.

Damn, she was hot.

So hot.

I turned the water on and yanked off my own t-shirt. Keeping my gaze glued to my mate, I quickly stripped. She grinned at me, fully naked and completely shameless and stepped into the shower.

It was hard to believe how lucky and unlucky I could be at the same time.

I had my mate here. Naked. Willing.

But she was human.

It went against nature that my wolf would choose her. An alpha wolf was always drawn to another alpha. The best of the breed. The strongest she-wolf who could produce future alphas for the pack.

Why in the fuck would my wolf pick her? It made no sense other than she met every one of my needs in bed… or the shower.

And yet, even as I questioned it, no part of me was disappointed in her. She was perfect. There was no question she was mine.

An alpha had to think about his pack. I had responsibilities that went far beyond what I wanted. I couldn't make a choice that would stamp out or lose the Wolf line of alphas and end our pack's autonomy.

I gave my head a hard shake. I didn't want to think about that—I couldn't. What guy would think about anything but the dripping wet naked woman in his shower? Right now, I needed to satisfy my mate. That was all that mattered.

I stepped into the shower after her and pounced.

14

WILLOW

If I'd thought Rob would be slow and tender in the shower, I would've been way off base. He was an animal. Even more feral than he'd been the first time. He claimed my mouth with urgency the moment he stepped under the spray, his lips suctioning over mine as his forearm scooped under my ass and lifted me into the air. I wrapped my legs around his waist, and he rotated and stepped forward until my back hit the shimmering aqua glass mini tiles.

I moaned into his mouth, kissing him back, my wet folds rubbing over the base of his cock. It was like TNT between us. Some kind of chemical formula that had two things coming together and forming an explosion. We were tame on our own—for the most part—but when Rob and I got together...

If ever a man had been worth my time, it was this one. He wasn't a quickie or a one-night stand. I couldn't stop thinking about him. Wanting him. Hell, needing what only he could give me. Yeah, he was a drug to me, and I was going to get another hit, right now.

He pinned me against the shower wall and ground his erection into me, his root rubbing my clit as I writhed against him. My legs went about his waist, my ankles hooking at his low back trying to get as close as possible.

"Not yet, angel. I need to taste you first," he rumbled, lowering my feet to the tile and sliding his palms down my slippery skin. He crouched in front of me, lifting one of my knees over his shoulder as he pinned my waist against the wall.

He gave a long lap over my slit as he looked up at me. "You wanna come fast or slow for your first time, angel?"

The sound of the waterfall shower was all that I could hear. But feel... I felt his tongue, his lips. His hands. I wanted his dick, too, but his mouth was wicked.

"Fast," I gasped. Because I was already desperate. I cupped my breasts, trying to ease the ache in them.

"Mmm." He nipped my nether lips. "I was just in this shower before you came," he said and nipped me again. "Thinking about you. About this." He made his tongue firm and penetrated me. "Jerking off to the memory of your glorious tits."

The image of him pleasuring himself in here—and recently—had me so hot I got dizzy.

I rubbed my eager flesh over his mouth, trying to get more friction. More action. More satisfaction. He found my clit with his mouth and swirled his tongue around it, grazed his teeth. And then he suctioned his mouth over the little nubbin.

I screamed, pulling at his hair. He had a talented dick *and* a talented mouth. My orgasm was swift and blinding—

running through me like a freight train. The heat from the shower made me dizzy, and the room spun. I would've fallen down if Rob wasn't still holding me up, still sucking on my sensitive bud, but gently now.

When it passed, I whimpered, my legs shaking.

Rob stood up, eyes—*yellow*.

Not brown. What the hell? I'd never seen anyone's eyes change so much in different light.

He cupped and played with my breast with one hand, still pinning me against the shower wall with the other. "Turn around, angel. I want to see that ass again."

I wasn't sure I was up for more anal—especially without lube, but the desire to obey Rob's hoarse commands and see how this played out was greater than any need I had to control.

I rotated to face the shower wall and spread my legs, looking over my shoulder for his reaction.

It didn't disappoint. Heat burned in his gaze as he stroked a hand down my side and over my ass. "Beautiful," he murmured. "You're so fucking gorgeous."

So much pleasure pumped through my system at that moment, I thought I'd overload... and I'd already come.

Rob reached out of the shower and retrieved a condom from the medicine cabinet. I turned my face back to the wet tile, listening as he ripped it open and rolled it on.

"I'm gonna fuck you right here," he rumbled, appearing right behind me, "so tomorrow when I'm in here stroking myself and thinking about you, I'll remember exactly how it feels to be inside you." He rubbed his cock over my slick entrance.

I was so ready for him. The anal had been amazing, and I loved that he'd gone straight to that yesterday—but right now my pussy wanted to be filled by him for the first time. Desperately.

I arched my back and pushed, taking him in.

He groaned as his thick length penetrated me and then inched in, deeper and deeper. My pussy was able to take him easier than my ass, but he was still big, and it was a tight fit. I was wet for him, and the orgasm had softened me up to accept him better. Still… I liked it big.

"This is all reward today, Natalie. You tell me how you like it," he rumbled.

The name *Natalie* grated on my ears like a betrayal, even though I was the one lying. I hated that in a moment like this, he wasn't saying Willow. He wasn't saying my name. It was as if all his potency, his virility and dominance wasn't for me. I was an imposter. Fuck, he didn't even know my name. Wasn't murmuring it in the throes of ecstasy. Using it to command me into positions.

But I couldn't think of that now. Not when he bottomed out in me with a slight bite of pain.

"I like this," I panted, my fingers splayed wide against the tile. I did. Hard. Deep. Rough. Wild. I loved everything he did.

He gripped my hips and glided slowly in and out. Every stroke was a wave of sensation. I panted just to assimilate it all. His size, his angle, how good it felt to have him so deep.

"More," I croaked when I'd grown used to it.

"Yeah?" He bumped into me harder.

"Yes," I encouraged. Damn, it felt good. It was hard to believe how good sex was with Rob Wolf. Beyond any other experiences I'd had.

His breath grew ragged, his grip on my hip bones bruising. He shifted his angle, so he could drive up into me, instead of straight in, and I cried out with the pleasure of it.

I loved feeling him so deep in me. Loved the wet sound of flesh against flesh, the feel of him pounding. Driving. Pushing me to take all of him.

Loved it.

"Yes, more," I crooned, even though it was already quite rough.

He braced his hand on the wall beside mine and jack-hammered into me, making my vision go hazy.

"More," I croaked again. I couldn't get enough, as if no matter what he did, I needed even more of him.

"Fuck," Rob muttered. He gripped my nape to hold me still and slammed into me with the upward thrusts that felt so good.

I moaned and sobbed with pleasure that built and built.

"I'm going to come," Rob warned. "I can't help it—you feel so good."

"I'm ready!" I cried out.

"Fates, yes," he roared. I barely registered the strange word choice because I was coming too, my channel squeezing and pulsing around his thick manhood. His breath felt warm on my shoulder, and I felt the scrape of his teeth against my skin before he abruptly pulled out and released me. The hot spray of the shower couldn't replace the warmth of his body.

"Whoa!" I moaned at the sudden loss of contact.

"Sorry," he muttered from the other end of the shower. "Hang on a sec, I'll... get cleaned up and find you a towel." He was facing away, cleaning up under the spray and disposing his condom.

His huge shoulders were bunched up in tight knots. I took a moment to admire him from the back—so muscular. Perfect.

I hadn't known I had a type, but I realized now, I did.

And he was it. A big strong cowboy. Manly but discreetly gentle. Rough in bed, cocky and dirty talking, but still kind and level-headed. Ridiculously smart, quietly observant.

At least that was my impression of him. I didn't know him that well yet. His sister-in-law's praise fit that view.

He turned off the water and left the shower without looking back.

It seemed strange, but I couldn't figure out why the sudden distance. Maybe he'd gotten dizzy with his orgasm too, and he was too much of an alpha male to admit any weakness.

That was probably it. He had stumbled back quite quickly. I could relate.

He reappeared in a moment with a towel spread wide for me. I stepped into it and let him wrap me up like a burrito.

Funny. I didn't usually let people take care of me. But with Rob, it didn't make me feel vulnerable. Maybe it was the sex that was making me weak. Making me... *gasp*, a girl.

I needed to get out of here. Sex with Rob was turning into more than a distraction. It was dividing my focus from why I was here. Not in Rob's bathroom but in Cooper Valley. Vaughn wanted me over at Markle's trying to get more information, and I'd already been screwing around—literally—with Rob for too long. I dried off and pulled on my clothes.

"Thanks." I stood on tiptoe to brush my lips across his. "I gotta get back to the house. Can I see you tomorrow?"

His eyes clouded at my manlike post-sex behavior, but he nodded. "Yeah. Tomorrow, when?"

"Um." I rubbed my lips together. I really needed to keep my schedule open for the investigation. It was my job, what I was being paid to do. Making social commitments would be a big mistake. "Can I call you?"

"Sure." Something in his tone told me he understood he was getting the brush-off and didn't much like it, but he took my phone when I handed it to him and entered his digits.

I texted him back, so he had mine—something I didn't usually do. I didn't want to be a jerk, so now he at least knew he could call me, too. I really did want to be with him. Hell, I wanted him to tug me to his bed right now for round two. I had to be level headed, at least for a little while. Focus on something besides mind melting orgasms.

"See you later, then." I picked up my bag with the pistol in it and left to find my way out.

Rob followed me down the stairs and out the door, being the perfect host and gentleman. He'd gone silent, but I got the feeling that he wasn't a man of unnecessary words. Except when it came to dirty talk. Then, he wasn't a gentleman at all.

"Bye." I turned around one more time to give him a kiss, and he snatched me up against his body and kissed me hard. It felt like a warning. Or punishment for leaving. Or... something.

A promise.

My toes curled in my shoes, and I came away breathless.

"See you later—tomorrow." Dang it— I sounded like a teenager. This guy was getting to me in a big way. I definitely needed some space to get my head back on straight.

I was here for a job.

A job.

Not to fall in love with the sexy cowboy next door.

15

WILLOW

I BLOW-DRIED my hair and freshened my lip gloss before I headed down to Markle's. I wanted to get a look in his outbuildings, but I doubted that was possible in broad daylight. I'd have to sneak back at night to see if I could get in although my plan was to watch for a pattern in the trailer shipments. Once I had enough intel, I could ask Vaughn for a warrant and bring in a team to search the place, but until then, I could find out more undercover. And that meant pandering to Markle's ego while my pussy ached from the pounding Rob gave it.

Rolling my eyes at myself in the mirror, I gave up. I was trying to keep him interested but not too eager that he'd think I wanted sex. I frowned as I went down the steps. He'd think I wanted sex with him because his ego was a mile wide.

This time, instead of cutting across the field, I drove. I

wanted an escape route in place and not on foot. It left me vulnerable to Jett's whims, and I liked having my Glock in the car.

Taking a deep breath and pasting on a fake smile, I rang his doorbell. The fancy sound of Pachelbel's *Canon* came through the door. Figured.

The door opened thirty seconds later. The cloying cologne preceded Jett.

"Natalie," he said. His smile wasn't as warm as before, so I laid mine on a little thicker.

"Hi. I wanted to say thanks for dinner the other night and wondered if you'd help me. I don't have a bottle opener." I held up a Chardonnay I'd found at the grocery store when I first arrived. I didn't take Jett for a beer drinker, and while he probably drank scotch, it was the expensive kind and my expense report probably wouldn't look good with a twenty-five-year-old bottle as a line item. Wine it was.

He studied the bottle and sniffed, not as if he was smelling it, but as if it were rancid. "Wolf doesn't have an opener?"

My heart thudded in my chest, but I'd been trained to keep my smile from slipping. "Wolf?"

"Rob Wolf." The words were followed by a sneer.

"What... what about him?"

"He should have a corkscrew... or is the only thing you're interested in getting from him a screw?"

"Jett... I don't know what you're—"

He held up his hand, and I instinctively stepped back with my right foot to make myself narrower, but also in readiness. He was an alleged middleman with connections to an international drug kingpin. On paper, Markle was clean. But he had a lot of land, though, to bury bodies.

"Stop. Cooper Valley's a small town. We're neighbors. There are no secrets here."

Besides the drug running he was doing after hours.

"Rob Wolf is just a friend," I admitted.

"Call it what he really is: a fuck buddy."

My cheeks burned hot from his insults… and the truth in his words. Rob was a fuck buddy. We hadn't stated we were anything more and, really? What else could he be? He thought I was someone else, and when he found out, he'd kick me out. That totally worked because I was leaving anyway, right after Jett was in handcuffs. Still, that stung.

"Rob means nothing. I'm here with you, now, aren't I?" I gave him a coy smile.

He looked me over. "I don't take sloppy seconds from a Wolf."

Stepping back, he slammed the door in my face.

Oooooookay. That went badly. My target, who I was supposed to get all hot and heavy with, thought I was a slut.

I walked back to the car realizing I probably was. No, I wasn't sleeping around—I liked sex, and I liked it naughty—but I was monogamous. Markle saw it differently. Starting the engine, I slapped my hand on the steering wheel and groaned. I'd fucked up. Whatever the beef was between Markle and Rob had messed with my plan. No, I'd ruined it all by myself. I'd made an attachment. I had no idea what kind, but there was something between me and Rob. Admittedly but unsaid, something more than just unbelievable sex. I'd felt it and ran with it.

I should've steered clear and kept my eyes on Markle.

"Stupid hormones and sexy cowboys," I grumbled as I turned out of Jett's driveway and onto the dirt road. I pulled over to the side. The sun hadn't set yet, but it was behind the mountains, and the evening sky was soft and muted.

Crickets chirped through the open car window. The perfect Montana evening, and I was alone in a car on the side of a rural road.

I was such a fuckup. Behind me was the case that I'd probably blown. Vaughn had okayed the job because I matched the real Natalie Shefield but also because I could become friendly with Jett. Get on his property. Get close. Get *him.*

I grabbed my cell.

"Vaughn."

"Small problem," I said, staring out the windshield at a falcon circling high overhead on an updraft.

"What?"

"I'm not Markle's type."

I heard his sigh. "You've got to be shitting me. You're pretending. It's not the dating game. Fake it."

"I did. He's not interested." I wasn't telling him the reason why. What I did with Rob was none of his business. Vaughn was single. Who he fucked wasn't anything I wanted to know.

"I'm going to watch the place again later. We have the lead on the animal hauler."

"Canadian customs confirmed the eighteen wheeler you spotted passed the border crossing north of Shelby. There are a lot of rules for live animals headed to Canada, words like breeder cow and brucellosis came up in the report." He sighed again. "All I know is the transport happened as you suspected. Find a repeat."

"Yes, sir." I wasn't going to argue. He was technically complimenting me in a bassackwards sort of way.

He hung up. It was my turn to sigh as I headed toward my house. *Natalie's* house. The case was going to hell. At least I didn't have to kiss Markle again. As for Rob, I had no answers there. I wanted to be with him, to see him smile. To *make* him smile because I knew I could do it, and I had a feeling it was a rare thing.

As if my thoughts had conjured him, Rob was on the porch, leaning against the rail as I pulled up. I couldn't help a smile of my own at the sight of him. A crisp pair of jeans and a white t-shirt. A simple, but lethal, combination.

He took his hat off as he came down the steps and met me.

"Hi," I said, going up on tiptoes and kissing him. "I didn't expect you."

He didn't kiss back, only sniffed. Once, then again. "You left this at my place." He held up my earbuds for my phone. "I thought I'd return them." There was no smile on his face. "You were with Markle again."

Markle had confronted me about the same thing only minutes before. With him, I'd been a little worried I might get shot. With Rob, I was worried I might get my heart torn out. I wasn't sure which would be more painful.

He looked down at my hand.

"With wine."

Shit.

"What happened? He fuck you and forget about it?"

Okay, that pissed me off.

I wasn't a slut and two guys just accused me of being one.

"That's unfair," I snapped.

"You were riding my dick, at my house, a short while ago. I wasn't enough for you?" His jaw was clenched, every muscle in his body taut. It didn't matter whether I'd fucked Jett Markle six ways to Sunday or not. Rob thought I did. It *looked* like I did.

The way Rob had sniffed when I'd gotten close, I

smelled like I did.

"It wasn't a date. I went there as a neighbor," I said, trying to smooth things over.

"With wine."

"Nothing happened. He didn't even invite me in."

"I told you, I don't like the guy. I don't think he's safe. I wouldn't let Audrey or Marina near him."

I was glad to hear that.

"I told you I can handle myself."

"Right." He stared at me, then shook his head. "Okay. You do that."

He didn't say anything else, only cut across the field that separated our land.

Shit.

I wanted to tell him the truth. That I wanted nothing to do with Markle, but I had a job to do. Rob might hate the guy, but I wanted him behind bars. We were on the same side.

It didn't matter. I couldn't tell him. I'd already fucked up the case enough. It would be blown wide open if Rob knew. I'd be on the next flight to Phoenix to clean out my desk, and Markle'd be on the next flight to a country without extradition to the US.

While something inside of me ached for me to call out to Rob, to follow him, chase him down and climb him like a tree, I couldn't.

This was the wakeup call I needed. I was Willow Johnson, DEA agent. I was assigned to find evidence to arrest Jett Markle and a connection to Murrieta.

And I knew better than to get involved with people under false pretenses. It only led to hurt. I never should have started anything with Rob Wolf.

Trouble was, now that I had, I didn't want it to end.

16

ROB

I WOKE in just as shitty a mood as I'd gone to bed. It had been two days since I discovered Natalie had gone over to Markle's house with a bottle of wine, I'd had to shift and run off my aggression on the mountain. I'd never been possessive of a woman before, but the pendulum swung the other way now. I was obsessed with her to the point of insanity, with moon madness tearing at me. She was my mate. What the fuck was she doing with Markle? He'd put his cattle on Natalie's land. Big deal. He'd even shot one of the pack. James had healed. But I wasn't going to recover if my mate ended up choosing Jett Markle over me.

I'd pushed myself hard, my wolf trying to burn off some of the anger, running until my paws ached, then crashed in my bed long after midnight. Yesterday, I'd thrown myself into work, rearranging all the hay bales in the barn just to keep my body moving. I'd been at it until late, then had gone straight to bed. This morning, I still had enough rage in me to snarl at anything that got in my way.

After showering in the place that reminded me way too fucking much of her, I dressed and stomped down the stairs to the kitchen. The house smelled sweet—Marina must already be up baking.

Damn, it was strange to have a female in the house. And a human, no less.

Because of Marina, Colton was a changed man—relaxed and happier than I'd ever seen him. I found them both in the kitchen. Colton sat at the table drinking coffee and eating a delectable-looking Danish and Marina was pulling a cookie sheet of croissants out of the oven. They both looked up at me as I stalked in and poured myself a cup of coffee.

"Late night?" Colton asked carefully. It was hard for any pack member to ignore his alpha's mood, and my frustration still simmered.

I just spat it out—no sense in trying to keep it in. "Natalie's still seeing Markle. She went over there yesterday with a bottle of wine."

"Oh," Marina said, eyes wide. She grabbed a plate, piled three different pastries on it and shoved it my way, as if sugar and carbs could make me feel better. "How do you know?"

"I was at her place when she came back, wine bottle in hand."

Marina tipped her head. She was a tiny thing, a disposition as sweet as her baked goods. Completely opposite from Natalie in every way.

"Empty wine bottle?"

I frowned. "No, unopened."

"So she didn't share a bottle of wine with him?"

I rubbed my unshaven face. Fuck, I really was going feral. "Well, no. She said she'd brought it over as a neighborly gesture, but he hadn't invited her in."

"So he didn't invite her in or accept the wine?" Marina clarified. She picked up the spatula and moved the cooling croissants to a platter. "I don't think that qualifies as seeing the guy. It sounds like, well, a neighborly gesture, like she said. If he didn't take it, he wasn't all that neighborly."

"You're saying what, exactly?"

"That he's as much of a jerk as we thought."

I looked to Colton. "If Marina took a bottle of wine to Markle as a *neighborly* gesture, would you lose your shit?"

He wiped his fingers with a napkin. "Markle's a dick. I don't want Marina anywhere near the guy."

"Exactly," I agreed.

"Natalie owns the house next door to him. They're going to be neighbors for a long time. She knows he put his cattle on her land without asking. She knows he's a dick. Maybe she's trying to smooth things over."

"You don't think she's trying to get in his bed?" I asked. The question made me sound vulnerable and weak. Natalie *was* my weakness.

Colton held up a hand. "I don't want to know the details of your sex life, but if you're a selfish lover and don't get her off, then I don't blame her for seeking orgasms elsewhere."

My wolf growled while Marina chided her mate. "Leave him alone. You Wolf boys would never leave a woman unsatisfied."

Colton grinned, stalked Marina around the counter until he got her in his arms and nuzzled her neck. She giggled.

I ignored them as I thought. Now that I told the story out loud and Marina repeated it back through her human female lens, and Colton made me feel like an ass, it didn't sound as bad as I'd taken it. Maybe this was one of those moments when I couldn't discern between my wolf instincts to claim and possess Natalie, to mark her forever with my scent so no other male ever touched her and what was normal human dating behavior.

Had I not pleased her sexually? I remembered what she looked, felt, smelled and even tasted like when she came. I hadn't skimped on the number of times I got her off. I was a generous, attentive lover.

But had I fucked up by acting too possessive? She didn't know she was my mate. She only knew we had chemistry and killer sex.

"Tell me you didn't go rip Markle's throat out," Colton said, his arms still around Marina.

"Oh, I wanted to, but I held back. Shifted and ran instead. I may have acted like a jackass with Natalie, though." I scratched the back of my neck, suddenly feeling less like an alpha and more like that jackass.

"Uh oh," Marina murmured.

I stared at the untouched plate of pastries without appetite. "It's probably for the best."

"What? That she hates you? Why's that?" Colton demanded.

"You know why. I've got Nathan Brown stirring up the goddamn pack so his kin can absorb us into theirs. I'm supposed to meet some pack princess from Canada in a couple weeks, and I don't really see how Natalie can actually be my mate."

Colton narrowed his eyes at me. "You're telling me you're not sure she's yours? You didn't know the moment you scented her?"

I ground my molars. "I knew," I growled, narrowing my eyes at him.

He stroked Marina's hair as he leaned against the counter. "Uh huh. So what part don't you believe?"

I sat back in my chair, overloaded with this untenable fucking situation. "Alphas mate alphas. It's the natural law. It just doesn't make sense that—" I cut off my words before I said something to offend Marina or Colton.

"It doesn't make sense that your mate would be human?" Colton supplied the hard edge to his voice, a warning.

"Not *your* mate." I glanced at Marina who gave me a smile. She knew what I was getting at. Colton was protective of his mate and their bond.

"Mine. I'm alpha. Things are different for me. You left, brother, for fourteen years. Boyd left for twelve. You're just getting a sense for what's going on around here. I've been the only Wolf on the ranch for a fucking long time."

Colton sighed, ran his hand through his short hair. I wasn't blaming him for going off and living his life. Mine though, was being alpha of this pack. I belonged here and only here. The needs of the pack came before mine.

"It shouldn't make a difference," he said.

"No, but it does. Am I making sense now? You heard about Nathan at the meeting. There's been undercurrents of that shit for years."

"Fate's a bitch, we all know that. But only when you fight her." He glanced down at my untouched food. "Eat your fucking pastries," he warned, like he was going to kick my ass if I offended his mate.

I picked up the warm croissant from my plate not because I was hungry but because I didn't want to be a dick and took a bite.

"Oh fuck, that's good," I exclaimed. The flaky croissant was filled with chocolate that melted in my mouth. "Wow."

"Right?" Colton said, grinning.

"You can take some to Natalie," Marina offered. "You know, as a peace offering."

Peace offering.

Fuck.

I had been a jealous dick the night before. I just couldn't figure out why a smart woman like her couldn't see Markle's true colors. Audrey had after one date with him. Maybe my perception was skewed by my wolf's need to mark her.

I should definitely stop by her place and apologize. I didn't know if bringing croissants was really my style, but my style seemed to have gotten me in the doghouse.

I could stop by her place after checking the fences.

And just like that, my appetite returned. I could grovel and so could my wolf in order to make things right. I'd told Natalie I was going to fuck things up. I had. She'd had warning, but it didn't make it right. She just needed to be prepared to forgive me. Often.

I shoved the other two pastries down my throat and downed my coffee, the anticipation of seeing Natalie again already changing my mood.

17

WILLOW

I ADJUSTED my camera's telescopic lens to get a closer view of the activity on Markle's property. From where I stood at the window of the master bedroom, nothing seemed out of the ordinary. I snapped some photos, just to document.

My search of Markle's barn and stable the night before had produced nothing. Nothing, which totally pissed me off. If he had more of the crates that had been loaded onto that cattle hauler, they were somewhere else.

Maybe the latest shipment had yet to arrive. I didn't know how the drugs arrived from South America to Markle's place. Catching that drop off would be huge.

When I'd done as much as I could from my location, I put on a pair of jogging shorts and runners. No one questioned a jogger running back and forth on their property. Besides, I needed a good run. I'd run cross country in high school, specializing in the longest distances until my foster parents made me quit because it took too much time away from my ranch chores. For some reason, I'd always had the endurance for running. Hell, I'd always needed it to stay sane.

After Rob stomped off last night, pissed, I'd been itchy and restless. He'd pretty much caught me red handed, and I didn't blame him for being mad. I wasn't a two-timer, but I'd certainly given him every indication I was one. It had been cruel. If I'd thought he'd been with another woman, I'd have ripped his throat out.

I knew it was for the best—I should let things fizzle out. That didn't stop me from planning to jog by Rob's place, too. If we accidentally bumped into each other and he was over being mad, I definitely wouldn't turn down the opportunity to explain as best I could without giving everything away. I wanted to spend more time with him, in or out of bed. I really liked the guy—it went beyond carnal attraction and good sex. He was definitely one of the good ones, as they said.

I put some sunscreen on my face and shoulders and stepped outside, breathing in the cool Montana air. It was a beautiful morning—not too hot yet. The smell of wild grass and pine cheered and relaxed me at once.

I put my earbuds in, the music setting a steady beat to follow and started jogging along the telephone line trail, then cut west down another path to check out Natalie's property line. As the current *homeowner,* it was up to me to see if any of her fences needed mending although it sounded like Rob and his brothers had been taking care of things like that. I didn't see a broken section, but I hadn't covered the entire perimeter of the property.

As part of my prep, the real Natalie had told me she'd

talked with Boyd Wolf a month ago, that they'd found her fence cut and Markle's cattle on her land.

The Shefield property was beautiful. Honestly, I thought I'd never want to see another ranch in my life after I left my foster home, but some silly part of me fantasized about staying here.

If I were the real Natalie, what would I do with the place? When I'd first arrived, my opinion had been she should do the repairs necessary to sell, to take the cash and run. Now? I wasn't so sure. Cooper Valley was gorgeous—the view of the mountains was breathtaking, and the big blue sky and open range gave a spaciousness to my thoughts and spirit I didn't find in Phoenix. Everything was so green. In the winter, it would be white, a frozen wonderland.

I was lost in those ponderings when I felt the hard pound of galloping hoofbeats. Tugging out an earbud, I heard a shout from the distance. "*Natalie! Stop*!"

I slowed, then stopped, even as it took me just a couple seconds to process that I was supposed to be Natalie. Rob was on a dark horse that galloped toward me at a breakneck speed, and he was pointing to my left.

I whirled and froze.

A bull, about fifty feet away, was squared off to me and running, horns lowered. The beast was black. Big. Pissed off.

Holy shit! Where the fuck had he come from? I got in a zone when running, but I didn't think I was so focused to miss a fucking bull. What in the hell was it doing on this property? Natalie didn't own a bull. Or cows.

I immediately knew.

Markle.

Mother. Fucker.

That asshole let his bull onto my—Natalie's—property. Whether it was to take advantage of this land or to get me back for being with Rob, I couldn't be sure. Right now, scrambling for my life, I felt pretty damn antagonized.

I veered right, not taking my eyes off the angry beast.

It ran straight for me, and it moved much faster than I could. I had to be quicker. My runners skidded in the dirt as I darted in the direction of Rob's approaching horse. Maybe he could somehow swing me up on the saddle with him, Wild, Wild West movie-style.

His horse whinnied and snorted as he approached, racing to get ahead of me and distract the bull. My heart pounded as I swerved and slid out in the dirt, falling onto one knee. I narrowed my eyes, trying to figure out which way to go to get away.

The bull ignored Rob and kept coming after me.

Then Rob did the stupidest thing possible, and swung off his horse, his boots landing hard in the grass. "Get on—get out of here!" He shouted, reaching for me. The bull turned around and came back toward us. It was almost upon us and the horse had taken off in fear, leaving us both behind.

Now there was nowhere for either of us to run. No tree to get behind. No fence to jump.

Where was my gun when I needed it? I didn't want to die like this. Seriously, it would be bad for my legacy, the DEA agent who'd been killed by a stupid bull in the line of duty.

A terrible, animal-like snarl came from Rob, coupled with the sound of tearing clothes and cracking bones. I'd had my gaze on the bull, and from the corner of my eye, pounced a huge wolf. The fierce animal attacked the bull, teeth bared, snapping for its throat.

I was cool-headed in emergencies. It was my job to keep my wits about me and do what had to be done. I'd been held at gunpoint. I'd seen sick fuckers do bad shit and took them down without even blinking. But I froze now, shocked by what I saw.

Rob's cowboy hat lay in the dirt at my feet.

A ripped pair of jeans and white t-shirt hung off that giant wolf's hindquarters as it chased the bull back, antagonizing it with ferocious nips on its shoulders, then flanks, as the beast spun and veered away.

What. The. Fuck.

The wolf remained, watching the bigger animal trot off, nose flaring and breathing hard. Finally, the wolf turned and loped toward me, its familiar amber eyes glowing bright.

I should be afraid. Very afraid. It was a fucking wolf.

And I wasn't.

I stooped to pick up Rob's cowboy hat, looking from it to the wolf as he approached. The animal was dark gray, the fur thick, a long line raised at the spine. It was huge—terrifying in size, especially after I'd seen those ferocious jaws snap. It body-checked my legs, making me stumble away from the bull, even though he was some distance away. Another body slam to move me, and then it showed its fangs.

I wasn't a screamer, but I definitely let out a breath with sound when it bit down on my...shorts. And tugged. Then released them and tossed its head in the direction of the horse who was now contentedly grazing on the tall grass far enough away not to feel threatened any longer.

"Okay, I'm moving. You want me to get the horse? Put the fangs away, wolf." Or did I mean, *Put the fangs away, Wolf?* I spoke cautiously, backing away in the direction of the horse standing a dozen yards away and keeping my gaze on both the wolf and the bull. The wolf faced the bull, as if standing guard in case it decided to charge me again. The bull looked at us, circling angrily, but not approaching.

I put Rob's hat on my head and picked up the reins. The horse was huge, but I managed to get one foot in the stirrup and stand in it, aided by a hold on the horn on the saddle, and swung my other leg over.

From the saddle, I sat and watched Rob—*in the shape of a giant, fucking wolf*—chase the bull back farther and farther until it bellowed and crashed through the wood fence onto Markle's land.

I kicked my heels into the horse's flanks and tugged the reins to turn back to Natalie's house. I hadn't been on a horse in a while, but it was like riding a bicycle. I never really lost the touch. Rob's animal was smart and knew exactly what I wanted him to do. When I got there, I dismounted and let the reins fall, giving the animal a quick pat on the neck. I went inside and grabbed my gun where I'd left it under the basket by the front door.

I walked back outside and aimed it at the wolf approaching the porch.

18

ROB

WELL, shit.

Having my mate point a gun at my chest was getting to be all too familiar.

I lowered my head and shifted back to human form—right there in broad daylight on Natalie's porch—something that went against every pack rule. Never show yourself to a human. Never let the secret out. She was pointing a gun at me and knew damned well how to use it. I needed to show her who I was before she shot me.

I hadn't meant to shift back there. I'd planned to distract the damn bull, but when it got too close and my mate's life was threatened, my wolf leapt to the surface without warning.

I hadn't even considered shifting. My wolf had made the choice all on its own.

The gun in Natalie's hand didn't waver, and she didn't

look surprised to see me rise to my full height and stand there, buck naked, except for the tattered clothes hanging off my limbs.

"Hold it right there." She sighted me over her left arm. She wasn't fooling around. "You're not coming any closer until you tell me exactly what you are."

She looked sexy as hell in her little running shorts and snug tank top. Her skin glistened with sweat and her hair, while pulled back mostly in a ponytail, was wild about her head.

I held out my palms. My cock had the unfortunate idea to get hard at the sight of my mate, such a beautiful badass in her fighter's stance and my hat on her head.

"Easy, angel." I advanced slowly. "I think you already know what I am. And you should also know that I'm no danger to you. I told you before I'd never hurt you. I'll always protect you from danger."

"You're a werewolf."

Slowly, I shook my head. "We prefer the term shifter."

Standing there silently, she studied me with those fierce green eyes. Considered. Finally, she glanced down at my boner and her lips twitched. She lowered the pistol and took my hat off with her right hand, then tossed it to me.

"Thanks." I used the hat to cover my jutting erection. "Can we step inside? I don't make it a practice to stand out in public with my dick swinging in the wind."

"Oh, I didn't see it swinging." A smile formed on her face as she backed into her house and let me pass. "Looked pretty sturdy to me."

"That's all for you, angel." I shut the door behind me and advanced on her.

She stopped retreating, letting me in close. She gripped my wrist and pulled the hat away from my crotch, guiding it up to my head instead. “Is this why you’re so big? Because you’re a wolf?”

“My dick?”

“All of you.”

I offered her a shrug and a small smile. I was reassured she hadn’t shot my ass, and I was inside, both good signs. I’d fucked up before. There was a chance I’d do so again. “Something like that.”

She peered up at me for a moment, then shook her head. “This is nuts. I don’t believe it.”

“I think you do. Question is, what are you going to do about it?”

She looked down at my erection and reached for it. Wrapped her fingers around the base in a firm grip. Stroked. “About this?”

I groaned.

I should’ve had a serious conversation with her. Answered every single one of her questions about what she’d just seen, what I was. Why. How. Everything. I should have made sure she wasn’t afraid of me. Made sure she wouldn’t tell anyone. But her little hand was short circuiting all brain power, so all I could do was choke out, “Yeah.”

“I can think of a few things.” She held my gaze as she slowly lowered to her knees. “Tell me you don’t turn into a monster at the full moon.”

My breath came out on a shudder as she flicked her tongue over the slit of my cock. “Not… not the way you think.”

“How, then?”

My abdominals flexed at the pleasure of her lips engulfing the head. I fisted a hand in her thick red hair. I forced my eyes to stay open, to watch as my dick parted her lips nice and wide.

"You'd have to tie me up to keep me off you." I resisted controlling her head, even though the need to pull that lush mouth all the way forward had my thighs shaking.

"Mm. That could be arranged," she murmured when she popped off and licked her lips. "But would I need to keep you off me? Why would I want to do that?"

I recognized that she was asking a real question, so I struggled to rein in control. I took a deep breath, let it out, even though I could barely process for the pleasure. "My only danger to you, Natalie, is lust. The full moon could make me get too rough in bed. I'm the pack alpha. The leader, which makes my strength and power even more intense. Plus, I'm... old for an unmated shifter."

She made a sound in her throat as she licked a drop of pre-cum from the slit.

"Fuck. I might... might want to mark you with my teeth."

Might. Understatement of the year. I was barely hanging on to control right now. The thought of tossing her over my shoulder, carrying her to the nearest horizontal surface and fucking into her as I sank into her shoulder rode me hard. It wasn't even the full moon... yet.

I gripped her wrists, kept them from touching me, so I could talk. My dick bobbed, angry and so hard it hurt, between us. I met her green gaze. "It's not like the movies. We don't roam the nights killing humans or turning them into our kind. We're just another species trying to keep from extinction. So, angel?"

"Yes?" Her eyes were wide, pinned on my face. I let go of her, and she took hold of my cock again, intent. I took a mental picture because it was one of the hottest things I'd ever seen.

"You can't tell anyone."

She nodded. "Okay."

Reaching out with as much gentleness as I could muster, I set my fingertips to her chin. "I mean it. No one. Not a soul. Do I have your word?"

She'd just found out the person who she'd been fucking was a shifter. I'd expected panic. Fear. Disgust. But she had my dick in her hand with a blatant plan to put it back in her mouth. And suck. "I promise. As long as your kind isn't hurting anyone, your secret's safe with me."

"We don't hurt. We protect," I explained. "As alpha, I set the rules. Enforce them."

"Of course, you're the alpha," she said.

"Angel, you need to know the truth, all of it. I want nothing between us. I hated keeping it from you because you deserve no secrets. I'm literally standing before you. Bare. Hiding nothing."

The smile fell from her lips and something shifted in her eyes, like her mind went somewhere else. It was quick, but I saw it clearly.

She had a secret, too. Something to do with that gun she carried.

But she wasn't ready to tell me.

Then her lips curved before she opened her mouth and took me deep, and I didn't care.

I choked on my breath, my eyes rolling back in my head. She knew the truth about me and still wanted me. Nothing could be more pleasurable than having my mate's mouth on my cock.

19

WILLOW

"I THINK I'm too old for the floor," Rob murmured, kissing the top of my head.

We were lying in the entryway, both of us naked now. I'd pretty much sucked Rob's balls dry, but his dick hadn't even flagged. Not one bit. He remained hard and stripped me bare before getting me beneath him, fucking me. Hard, quick, dirty. I had his cum dripping from me and down my thighs as I rested my head on his shoulder, his arm around me and caressing the skin on my hip.

I'd never gone without a condom before. Not until Rob. We hadn't used one when he'd fucked my ass the other day, but there'd been no worries about pregnancy with that. I was on the pill, so I had that covered after this latest round. I didn't think Rob was negligent. We had both been... feral.

So wild for each other we hadn't even thought about protection. Maybe that was what something so fierce as what was between us was about. It was mindless. So intense that all smart thinking fell away in tatters like his destroyed clothing. And mine.

He'd said he'd wanted no secrets between us. He'd told me he was a shifter. Part wolf. Nothing else he could say could be a bigger surprise. Maybe he killed a guy. Maybe he liked to wear women's panties on Saturdays. None of that was as big as what he'd shared with me. Sure, he'd shifted because of his protective nature, yet he'd exposed himself.

Me? I was the one who held all the secrets. I wasn't even Natalie.

"Want to try that again, in a bed?"

How could I do that, have sex which wasn't just sex, it was a *connection*, with a lie between us? How could I tell him the truth? It was a federal case I was involved in. I couldn't even tell my mother, if I had one.

And yet, I did want to try that again. In a bed.

"Food first." I was starving.

"I have no clothes here. I'm not sure if cooking naked is a good idea."

"Walking home naked is?" I countered.

"I'll stay here until dark, then shift and run home."

Something he'd said before made sense now with some context. "I'm guessing the dog Markle shot wasn't a dog?"

He moved me, so I lay mostly on top of him, one of my legs settling between his. He stroked back my hair from my face. I had no idea where the hair tie went, but I had no doubt it was a wild snarl now.

"It was one of the younger wolves—just a teen—cutting across your property to meet a girl."

I couldn't help but grin. "You shifters are a randy bunch." Another thought came to me. "Audrey came by the other day. Is she—"

"No. She's Boyd's mate. Wife, too. She's human like you. Her sister, Marina, is mated to Colton."

"Mated?"

His skin beneath me was almost hot to the touch. I swirled my finger through his chest hair.

"When a shifter finds the female for him, they mate."

"Is that a kinky word for sex?"

"It's a permanent bond, a lifelong one. Mating occurs during sex when a male bites his mate."

My mouth fell open, and I met his gaze. "That's why you said you'd want to mark me with your teeth."

He blinked. "Yes. It embeds our scent into the female's skin, so the other males will know she's been claimed."

"And the full moon...makes you want to mark a woman?"

He shook his head. "Only one. You only get the urge to mark the female your wolf chooses."

I swallowed. "And you have that urge with me."

I caught a vulnerability in his gaze—the first time I'd seen him anything but strong. He nodded. "My wolf chose you."

Oh my God.

"Oh my God," I whispered. He wanted to *mate* me? As in a lifelong, permanent bond? With *me?*

"I... I don't know what to say. I mean it's—"

He put a finger over my lips. "Don't freak out. It's too much to take in all at once."

"So, what makes the wolf choose?"

He shrugged. "No one knows. Fate, I guess."

I suddenly recalled his use of the word *fate* during sex when we were at his place. Like a curse word. Or praising a deity.

"So, what happens if your wolf chooses someone you can't stand?"

His laugh was explosive. Hearty.

I absolutely loved hearing the rich baritone.

"Impossible. She might drive you fucking nuts. She might even point a gun at your chest every time she sees you," —he winked at that— "but you find it all utterly intoxicating."

I couldn't scarcely breathe. "So... you're intoxicated? By me?"

"Yes."

"What happens when it wears off?"

"Wolves mate for life. A she-wolf could leave her mate, but he'd always follow. He'd always have the need to protect her. To provide for her. He'd try to fix whatever went wrong."

"Sounds a little stalker-ish."

Rob grinned. "Yeah, I guess it might. There are bad matches sometimes. The greater danger to our species is not finding your mate."

I went still. "What do you mean?"

"An unmated male could go feral. We call it moon madness. He gets stuck in wolf form and can't change back. Then he'd have to be put down to protect the pack."

A shiver went up my spine. "Are you saying if we don't do this... mate thing, you'll go mad?"

He was quiet for a minute as he studied a lock of my hair. "Not necessarily. Let's not get ahead of ourselves. You just found out what I am." His hand slid down my back and cupped my ass. His fingers slid over my pussy, and I felt a growl rumble from his chest.

"I love feeling my cum slip from you."

I set my head on his chest, listened to his heart beat as he ran his hand over me, up my spine, over my bottom again, and then back between my thighs.

He'd have to be put down.

Rob could die all because I couldn't mate him.

I couldn't do it. I had a job in Phoenix. I wasn't Natalie Shefield. I wasn't even the person his wolf needed. He couldn't be stuck with me forever. Well, his forever would be short because he was going to *die.*

If there was another woman, someone else who his wolf liked, then he could mate her and wouldn't die. The idea of him laying like this with another woman made me want to claw her imaginary eyes out.

"Shh," he crooned, and his fingers slipped between my thighs to play. "I can practically hear your mind working. Don't worry about me, angel. I'm the alpha of the pack. The alpha of you, too. I handle all the worries."

I let out a puff of air at that. Ridiculous man—wolf. I didn't mind his alpha male assertions though. All the men in law enforcement were alpha types. I was completely used to their style, and in my opinion, Rob wore it best of all the men I'd known. I wiggled my hips because his touch, remarkably gentle for everything we'd done together, was getting me going again. Especially since it was his cum that was making me so slick.

"Rob..."

"Let me play now." He rolled us, so he was on top and slid down my body, nudging my legs wide as he went.

I pushed at his head. "Rob, I'm all messy."

He looked up at me from between my thighs. He ran a finger through my trimmed patch of curls above my clit. "I like red here. Let me play. I love the scent of us together. Knowing you're marked by me. This pussy is mine, angel. Any shifter will scent me on you now."

He licked me, and I forgot everything. Only Rob. Only what he was giving me. I blinked my eyes open and stared at the ceiling as he ate me out. He was giving me everything, and even though I'd sucked his dick, I couldn't give him what he really wanted. All of me. The *real* me.

Even I didn't know who that was. I wasn't Natalie Shefield. I wasn't even Willow Johnson, for that was the name a social worker gave me when I first went into the system.

I might be a mate to Rob, but I was one hundred percent a lie.

20

ROB

I CAME in from the stables a week later to find Marina whipping up a storm in the kitchen. Colton and Boyd were both at her mercy, her calm orders getting them to do her bidding. *Get the eggs from the fridge. Fill the big pot with water to boil. Not that platter. The big one.*

Audrey sat at the table peeling potatoes. She didn't look too thrilled, and as she was the first to admit she couldn't cook, it was probably safest for her with a table between her and the sharp knives. While she could wield a scalpel in the operating room, she couldn't chop onions without disaster.

"Where's your phone, asshole?" Boyd demanded. He glanced up from the sink where he was filling a pot. "You haven't returned any of my texts."

I checked my back pocket, found it empty, then groaned. "I don't know. I must've left it at Natalie's last night." The thing was probably dead by now.

For the past week, I'd spent all my spare hours over at the Shefield place. My wolf was happy. I was happy. My dick was happy. Natalie's pussy was *very* happy. I made sure of it. While I was with her, I almost forgot that I was alpha. I thought of myself as her man. Her mate.

She wasn't a wolf, so she didn't understand the dynamics of me being alpha. Didn't understand the importance of it, of what her role would be if she were the alpha's mate. Some female shifters had wanted to be my mate for status alone, not for me. I'd learned that early on, still a teenager. A hard lesson, but I'd been careful ever since. I wasn't keeping my position from her, but it didn't really come up. Pretty much the only thing that *did* come up for the time we were together was my dick.

She wasn't big on sleepovers, and I didn't push, just spending evenings over there. She was fiercely independent —I had to respect that and take things slow although the closer it got to the full moon, the stronger my need was to mate her.

Alphas didn't stop being alphas because of being side-tracked. It all came down to pussy. Sure, it was a crude term, but I loved Natalie's. But I still had some pack princess from Canada coming down to meet me, and everyone wanted me to fall in love with her pussy. To be so obsessed with it that I'd sink my dick in it and bite her and end my moon madness once and for all. Or so they believed.

I didn't want the pack princess. Hell, I didn't even know her name. I wanted Natalie, and I had no fucking idea how to make it work. I had shit to figure out if I was going to actually claim her when she was ready.

After it got dark each night, I shifted and ran in the hills to ease my mounting aggression before heading to my shower and bed. Alone. It was for the best because as the full moon drew closer, my urge to mark her grew stronger. But it wasn't just that.

I wanted her here in this kitchen now. Part of the family. I wasn't sure how I was going to pull it off, but it was impossible to doubt how perfect it would be.

Why would my wolf choose a human if it wasn't meant to be?

"What's going on?" I asked, grabbing a glass from the cabinet and filling it with ice and water from the dispenser in the fridge door.

"Picnic. We thought we'd have a pack potluck, so everyone could meet Natalie," Marina said, chopping celery on a wood cutting board. "Audrey stopped by on her way back from the store and invited her."

I paused, mid-drink. "Why would the pack want to meet Natalie?"

Maybe it was the low tone of my voice or the fact that I spoke very slowly that had Colton stepping in front of Marina, shielding her from me.

"She's your mate, you dumbass," Colton said. Since he was now out of the military, and he was getting it on the regular from Marina, my brother was more relaxed than I'd ever seen him. Except now when his mate was threatened.

I wasn't going to hurt Marina. Colton knew that, yet still, his mate instincts were strong.

She pushed him out of the way. "I'm not afraid of the alpha. I'm armed, remember?" She waved the knife, rolled her eyes and went back to the celery.

"I know Natalie's my mate. You four know. Clint, too. But I don't want the whole pack to know. Boyd, you were at the meeting last week. You saw what a fuck-up that turned out to be."

"We're not telling anyone she's your mate," Boyd said.

"She's the new neighbor. And she's old man Shefield's great-niece. Most of the pack remember Mr. Shefield, and it's neighborly to have her over. I'm sure she'd like to hear all the good things everyone has to say about her kin."

When he put it that way, I felt like an asshole. I took a big swig of my water, then put the glass in the top rack of the dishwasher. Leaving it for Marina to put away would only make me more of a dick.

"You're right," I sighed. "That is a good idea. It would be odd if we didn't."

"I was thinking of having the Barn Cats come and play," Boyd added. "Our wedding reception was cut short because of the storm. When I talked with Natalie on the phone before she moved, she said she was a concert violinist. You remember Shefield was a fiddle player. I'm thinking that was what she had in common with him—why he left her the place."

That's right. I'd spent a full week with Natalie, and she hadn't shared anything about that part of her life. Sure, I knew she had thirty-seven freckles on her shoulder, and her left nipple was more sensitive than the right. Music? It hadn't come up. She'd been as sidetracked as me.

"Call her, Rob," Audrey said, setting her peeled potato in a bowl and grabbing another. She glanced at Marina. "How much potato salad do we need?"

"Ten pounds."

"I thought this was a potluck," she grumbled.

"It is. Keep peeling. The exercise is good for the baby."

Audrey laughed, then looked at me again. "Call Natalie and tell her to bring her violin. Fiddle. Whatever it's called. She could play with the Barn Cats. It'll be fun to watch and a great way for her to fit in."

I reached for my phone in my back pocket, then remembered. “Shit. No phone.”

“I’ve got her number.” Boyd pulled his cell out. “I called her last month before she moved with the update about Markle’s cattle.”

I remembered that fiasco well. Markle was a dick through and through, taking it upon himself to use Natalie’s grazing land without her consent.

“Great,” I said, holding out my hand for it.

He held the phone out of reach. “I’ll call her,” he said with a grin. “You’d better hop in the shower. You know how the pack likes to show up early.” He sniffed. “You smell like a horse.”

“Horse’s ass,” Colton murmured.

I gave my brothers a death glare.

“All right.” I headed up the stairs after whacking Colton on the back of the head.

“Hey, Natalie, it’s Boyd Wolf. You won’t believe how many potatoes Audrey’s peeling…”

I didn’t hear the rest of my brother’s conversation with Natalie. I just knew I’d see her again in a few hours. I got hard as I walked up the steps. Just thinking about seeing her turned me on. It was a good thing I was headed for the shower. I could take care of the problem. My fist wasn’t as good as Natalie’s pussy, or mouth… or ass, but it would have to do until later.

21

WILLOW

I SHOWED up at the Wolf Ranch carrying a tray of deviled eggs. I wasn't much of a cook, but that was the thing my foster mother had always brought to potlucks, so it seemed like the thing to do.

I'd hated these get-togethers as a kid, always feeling out of place. I was just another one of the Johnsons' many foster kids that everyone kept a sharp eye on because we couldn't be trusted with their children or their things.

I didn't particularly want to be at this one, either.

No, that was a lie. I liked being here.

Too much. I liked the closeness of Rob's family. The way they seemed to have each other's backs.

The past week with Rob had been delicious. Sinfully delicious. But the whole time, I'd known they were stolen moments. I couldn't have Rob Wolf.

Being here with his incredible family and pack made that painfully obvious.

I didn't belong.

I was living a lie. Rob needed to mark a female before he succumbed to moon madness. I knew he believed his wolf had chosen me as his mate, but I suspected that was just biology talking. Like how human females had the biological clock thing going. When they reached the end of their breeding window, they got kind of desperate and married any guy they thought would make a decent father.

Rob had the same thing going. It was his time, and I'd moved in next door. Our chemistry was off the charts, so he was sure I was the one.

But I knew that was impossible.

I was living a lie, and when he found out I wasn't Natalie, that I was here under false pretenses, he was going to be pissed. No apology would take back that sense of betrayal he would feel.

I shouldn't have let us get this close—the situation was a guaranteed heartache for both of us.

"Hey, you must be Natalie," a pretty young woman said, taking the tray of deviled eggs from me. "I'm Marina, Audrey's younger sister."

Much younger. I was surprised.

"Nice to meet you." I followed her to the back yard where a barbecue grill was already smoking with the scent of searing meat.

My mouth watered. "Oh my God, is that peach pie?"

Marina beamed. "It sure is. Baking is kind of my thing."

"Hey there. You must be Natalie." Two good-looking younger cowboys sauntered up to me. "I'm Rand," one of them said. "And I'm Nash," the other finished.

"They're ranch hands here at Wolf Ranch," Marina supplied.

Apparently, all the cowboys at Wolf Ranch were very fine specimens of manhood, not that these two held any candle to Rob.

Rob showed up and reached for my hand, tugging me against him in a hug. "There you are."

I noticed a number of heads turned as people stared at me. I pulled away from Rob, my defenses going up.

"The pack will love you," Rob reassured in a low voice. "Your great-uncle was a friend to many here." But then he pulled away and rubbed his face. "They just may not love the idea of me mating you."

"Let's not go there, then," I said quickly, taking a step back and putting more distance between our bodies.

I couldn't mate this guy. Did he think I could?

Why then, did having my body apart from his set off a sense of yearning that made my whole body ache?

"Right," he agreed. "We'll keep what's between us private for now." For a moment, I caught the hint of unhappiness in the lines of his face. The weight of responsibility for his brothers and the whole pack on his shoulders.

I squeezed his arm, the ache in me growing stronger. Rob was an amazing man. Selfless and giving. Strong and protective. And this life he had here on the ranch—I never thought I'd want something like this. My childhood had been so shitty. But now that I was here, now that I got to see what he had—the sense of community, of family—now it felt like exactly what I craved. The refreshing antidote to my childhood. A redo on a beautiful Montana ranch filled with kindness and love.

And really hot kinky sex.

Too bad none of this was real.

"So, Rob," an older man came up and thumped Rob on the back. "When is the contingent from Canada showing up? Do you have any events planned?"

I didn't know what they were talking about, but the detective in me didn't miss the way Rob's jaw clenched and the quick—and guilty—look he darted my way.

"I'll be right back, Natalie," he said, stepping farther away with the man, like he didn't want me to hear.

"You're not worried about that situation, are you?" Marina appeared at my elbow, speaking in a low voice.

I turned to face her fully. "What is the situation, exactly?"

She flushed. "Oh—um—it's nothing," she stammered. "Just some visitors that are coming."

"What visitors?" I demanded. "Why would I be worried?"

Marina grabbed my arm and tugged me away from the crowd. "It's this stupid thing," she explained in a quiet voice. "The pack elders wanted Rob to meet some alpha female in case he wanted to mate her. They don't know about you because Rob was kind of giving you time to adjust to the whole shifter thing. Plus... they don't exactly love the idea of us humans mixing in." She shrugged. "Don't let it bother you. Rob's alpha. He can do whatever he wants."

That wasn't true. I knew it as soon as I heard the words. A dictator did whatever he wanted. A leader didn't. He had a responsibility to his pack. And Rob was definitely a leader. The kind who put the good of all in front of his own. So that's why he looked so strained over the pack knowing we were dating.

Even though I'd known this thing with Rob couldn't work, some part of me still resisted the obvious answer—

telling him we couldn't be and letting him have at it with the alpha she-wolf.

In fact, the idea of Rob being with her made me want to throat punch the woman.

Crap. Every day this got harder and harder. It was like a train running at top speed toward the car on the tracks. I knew there would be a crash, I just didn't know how to stop it.

22

Rob

We were nearing the full moon, but this wasn't a get together to shift and run in the moonlight. Instead, it was an afternoon picnic. By five o'clock, about twenty pack members were in the field behind the house. Usually, we met in the barn, so there was some shade and a roof in case it rained, but the construction project wasn't finished. Sawhorses with boards across were set up as tables for the hefty quantity of food everyone brought. From Marina's and Audrey's potato salad to peach pie, hamburgers and even homemade ice cream had been devoured. The Barn Cats were tuning their instruments and setting chairs beneath a tree where they'd perform. Some laid out blankets, so they could sit and listen. Others had brought fold-up chairs.

Natalie sat beside me in a pretty green sundress that matched her eyes and had me wanting to slip the little straps off her shoulders and devour what was beneath. I'd kept as close as I could to her since she arrived. As close as I could without raising questions from the pack. I now wished I'd cancelled this BBQ before it started because being near Natalie without showing the whole pack she was mine fucking killed me.

People had, just as my brothers and their wives had assumed, regaled her with stories about her great-uncle. He'd been a kind, patient human who always had time for the pack. While no one had told him we were shifters, it was assumed he knew and didn't care. The tales were all good ones, and hopefully, Natalie could cherish them.

"The Barn Cats are ready for you," Boyd said, coming up with Audrey tucked under his arm.

"What? Me?" Natalie asked, looking at my brother in confusion.

"Yeah, you brought your fiddle over, didn't you?"

When she continued to stare at him blankly, he cocked his head, narrowing his eyes slightly. "We talked about it on the phone earlier."

I thought I detected alarm in her expression before she smoothed it out. "Oh, right. Yes. When we talked on the phone."

"So, where's the fiddle?" Boyd glanced around. "Got your case stored somewhere?"

She frowned. "Um, no. Sorry, I forgot it. I guess Rob's addled my brain."

"It's all right if you forgot," I reassured her. She seemed strangely uncomfortable, which made my wolf extremely protective.

Boyd put his fingers in his mouth and an ear-splitting whistle cut through the air. Everyone turned to look our way. "Kurt, got an extra fiddle? We've got an extra fiddle player right here." Boyd pointed down at the top of Natalie's head, and everyone started to clap and cheer.

All color bled from her cheeks, and she took a step back.

"What's the matter?" I asked, leaning in so only she—and every other wolf around—could hear.

"I'm not in the mood to play."

Boyd took his arm from around Audrey, then slung his other around Natalie, as if taking on a new mate. "Nonsense, they play easy stuff in comparison to what you're used to. Don't worry, they won't be pulling out any Mozart. Come on, darlin'. Show 'em what you got. Don't be afraid. From what we talked about last month when you were still at school, you're a hot shot player."

Natalie offered him a fake smile, but he gave her no choice, leading her through the small group of pack members to the other musicians. They introduced themselves one at a time, then Kurt handed her a violin and bow. The old guy was as grizzled as they came, but he was a mean fiddle player and had a kind soul.

I had no idea what the difference was between a violin and a fiddle, but I knew I liked the sound either way.

Natalie didn't sit down, so the guys didn't either. They moved to stand, so she was in the center of them, five musicians lined up. Kurt began to play a lively melody, the other Barn Cats picking up the tune.

Pack members clapped and stomped their feet. Natalie smiled nervously, then looked around. Then she set the bow and fiddle down on a table, reached for a can of soda, put it to her mouth, and spilled it all down the front of her.

Purposely.

Something was off.

"Oh God," she murmured with a forced laugh. "I need to

go clean up." She set the violin gently back in its case and made a beeline toward the house.

I intercepted her on the way, taking her hand and leading her through the back door and into the house. Shifters had exceptional hearing, but hopefully they wouldn't eavesdrop from in here. It was one thing for the entire pack to know my business, it was another for them to overhear it.

"Angel, you want to tell me what in the hell's going on?"

"Nothing. I just spilled." She grabbed some paper towels from the roll and dabbed them over the soda on her dress. "I should probably get home and change."

"Bullshit." I caught her arm and turned her to face me.

She tensed into what I would swear was a fighter's stance—her knees soft, her elbows loosely bent. I caught the scent of fear, and it turned my stomach sour.

My mate was afraid?

Of me?

Something wasn't right here. I could sense it, being alpha. It made for a great leader the fact that I had a very strong bullshit meter.

Why wouldn't she want to play with the others? It was obvious she didn't. Nothing made sense. My mind raced over the possibilities.

"We didn't talk much about your schooling. After a week together, that makes me an asshole, and I'm sorry for that. Did something happen that you don't want to play anymore?"

She shook her head and went over to the center island. She picked up an apple from a bowl, clearly fidgety. "I don't want to mess up in front of all your friends and family."

I smelled another lie.

My mate was lying to me. *Again.* My wolf howled with dismay.

I was right. Something was wrong. Natalie wasn't shy. I doubted since she was getting a Master's degree in music she'd have stage fright. It was as if—

Boyd walked into the kitchen. I glared at him, wanting him out, but he folded his arms over his chest and walked over to flank me.

Like he would if I were under threat.

But by Natalie?

"So, you forgot the fiddle?" Boyd asked. The question definitely sounded aggressive. My wolf didn't like it, but a prickle of foreboding had already begun at the base of my skull. Boyd knew more than I did, it seemed. I just had to wait it out.

"Yeah." She gave a shaky laugh. "Sorry. The truth is, I got pretty burnt out on music in school. I don't ever want to play the violin again."

That was a different story than what she'd offered me a moment ago.

"Well, did you at least bring the mayonnaise?" Boyd demanded. "Remember, from when I called earlier?"

Natalie lifted her eyes from the apple. "What? Oh, gosh. Sorry! I guess I forgot that, too." She ran her fingers over her hair, then spun away.

I'd dealt with some bad shit with the pack over the years. Someone had hurt a kid once. That had been bad. Another drank himself off a bridge. But I had a sinking feeling that what was going to happen next was going to destroy me. I couldn't figure out what, exactly, but if Boyd was here questioning her, he was doing it for a reason. He wasn't accusing her of anything. It was more like he was trying to pull answers from her. To gauge her response. I'd done it many a time, setting a trap for someone to step in and...

"On the call, I didn't ask you to bring mayonnaise," Boyd said in a low, dangerous tone.

Natalie went still, her gaze narrowed. I'd seen her pissed at me before, deservedly so. This was all defense.

"Tell me, *Natalie,* who the fuck did I talk to this afternoon?" Boyd asked. "Because it sure as hell wasn't you."

Her cheeks flushed a pretty pink, but this time not because I'd brought her to orgasm.

Her jaw clenched in defense, but tears popped into her eyes. She blinked them back. I hated when females cried, especially my mate, but I wasn't going to hold her now. She was holding onto something. A secret. A big fucking secret.

When she didn't answer, I slapped my hand down on the counter. "Who did Boyd talk to?" I put alpha power into it without meaning to. Both she and Boyd drew back.

"Natalie," she blurted. "He spoke to Natalie."

"You."

Her fiery curls swayed as she shook her head. "The real Natalie."

I took a step back as I stared at my mate before me. A tear slipped down her cheek, but she remained silent.

"Who the fuck are you, and what have you done with Natalie Shefield?"

She inhaled and let out a long breath. "Natalie is in LA. She's fine. I didn't kill her and stuff her body in a freezer." She looked at Boyd, then at me. "My name is Willow Johnson. I'm a DEA agent, and I'm here undercover."

My eyes flared wide, and my wolf wasn't sure if it should howl in misery or snap at her at her deceit.

"We don't have drugs here. You've done a thorough

check of my bed. Search the rest of the property, then get the fuck out." I pointed at the closed door.

The tears came faster now. "You're not who I'm investigating."

"Oh no?" I asked. I'd never hit a female before, and I wasn't going to start now, but this woman... this imposter... was trying my abilities to hold back. She'd tricked me and my wolf. She wasn't Natalie Shefield. All this time, I'd had no idea. What a pathetic alpha I was.

"It was all a lie, wasn't it?" My brows went down low. "Were you using me to get information? Was any of it real?"

"Rob, no—"

"Fuck, I opened up to you." I took a step toward her when I realized something. "Holy fuck. You know the truth about the pack."

It was my job to protect the shifters who looked to me to lead, and I'd broken the biggest secret of all. No one could know we were shifters. I didn't just tell the hot neighbor. I told a fucking DEA agent. Not only did I have moon madness and my wolf had chosen a human... a lying human, but I'd blabbed pack details like a middle school girl.

"I won't tell your secrets, Rob," she whispered.

"Says the liar," I snapped.

She flinched at the words.

I took a step closer and pointed at her. "You mess with my brothers, my pack... any shifter, I'll know. As alpha, I have the responsibility to protect everyone and that includes eliminating all threats."

"Rob..."

I didn't give her the chance to talk. She'd had days. *Days* to tell me the truth.

"Get the fuck off my property before anyone else finds out you're a fake. They won't be so kind. Trust me."

I didn't say anything else, only turned my back on her, just as she had me. My wolf may have thought Natalie was my mate, but he was wrong. The woman who was walking through the house to the front door wasn't even Natalie Shefield.

"Rob," Boyd said, but I held up a hand to keep him silent.

I listened for her car to pull away, but before it did, I heard another arrive. We followed Natalie's—no, Willow's—path to the front porch. Three men and a beautiful young woman piled out of a big truck with Canadian plates.

"Alpha Wolf?" the man rumbled.

I couldn't focus on him because Natalie—fuck!—Willow was standing with her car door open, leaving. I stared at her, my chest ripped open and bleeding onto the ground.

"Yes?"

"I'm Alpha Jackson, from Manitoba. This is my daughter Kara."

Oh, for fuck's sake.

This night couldn't get any worse.

23

WILLOW

I STOOD ROOTED to the ground, staring at the beautiful alpha wolf meant for Rob. The one Marina had told me about.

Oh God.

This was the train wreck I saw coming.

Rob wasn't looking at her, though. He was looking at me—the pain of betrayal burning in his gaze. I'd made him look at me that way. It was my own doing.

I scrambled into the car and rushed to start it. I had to get away. Leave him to get on with his life. I backed up fast, tires skidding the dirt, then took off for home.

Home. Ha. What a joke.

I tried to stay strong, but halfway back to the house, I broke down and cried the whole rest of the short drive. It was any wonder I didn't end up in a ditch. Everything I'd thought would happen, had. Rob learned the truth and felt slighted. No, that wasn't the right word. Betrayed.

He'd bared his soul, and that of his community, to me, and I'd given him nothing in return. Only lies.

Not everything had been fake though. How I felt about him and how I showed it hadn't been pretend. I felt for Rob. Deeply. For once in my life, I cared for someone else. I cared that I'd hurt him, that my real life had ruined the only good thing that had ever happened to me.

I'd been on my own for so long, I didn't even know I was able to fall for a man. I'd thought I was unlovable. Unwanted. I'd never been adopted, only coasted through my entire childhood in the system, at the whims of selfish adults who only wanted me for the money I could bring them from the state.

I'd built a wall around my heart, a wall so big that it had kept me safe from hurt, otherwise I'd have crumbled so long ago. I'd thought love made one weak. In fact, loving Rob had made me strong. I hadn't had to rely on myself. I'd trusted.

I'd destroyed that, though, all by myself.

I turned off my car and stared at the Shefield house. I was becoming charmed by the old quirks of the place. The slanted porch floor, the old windows that took muscle to open. Every door in the house squeaked. It was... charming. Unique, as if it was a living thing. *A home.*

Up until I'd driven into Cooper Valley, my job as a DEA agent had been my life. Rob made me realize there was more to me than just my badge. In fact, he hadn't even known I was law enforcement. He'd shown me all the dark and empty corners that had been waiting to be filled.

God, the picnic today had been incredible. And scary. Everyone there belonged. Not everyone was related by blood but a bond of being shifters. There was no question they were a family in their own special way. They took care of each other. Protected. Lifted up. Helped.

They'd welcomed Audrey and Marina, and they were human. They were quickly incorporating me into their group as Mr. Shefield's relative. He'd belonged, so I belonged, too.

That welcoming spirit was uncomfortable to me. I wasn't used to the idea of immediate acceptance. Even within the DEA, one had to earn respect and friendship. My job depended on the outcome of the Markle case. If I failed, I'd be moved to some crap work detail. There was no allegiance, no bond. My role would be filled by someone else. Immediately replaced and forgotten.

Vaughn was getting antsy with my lack of momentum on the case. I'd figured out the outgoing drugs, but the incoming… nothing had happened for a week. Had I been wrong or were they taking their time?

I climbed from the car and went up the steps to the front door.

The same would be said for the Wolf pack. My role as Rob's female was to be replaced by someone else.

How timely.

The Canadian female wolf with long dark hair, olive complexion, high cheekbones, lush curves. Young. Probably a virgin who Rob could mold to his every desire. Who was probably ridiculously fertile and would give him a shifter baby on the first go.

I'd scratched an itch. Lots of itches, but nothing more. I wasn't perfect. I had a past that was tainted and made me… defective. Rob was better off without me. As alpha, he had to be proud of his mate, and surely, he hated my guts.

My phone buzzed, and I saw a text from Vaughn. *Natalie Shefield called to say Boyd Wolf called her about a BBQ.*

Yeah, no shit. Could've used that info a few hours ago, thanks.

I picked up my gun from the kitchen counter, checked the magazine even though I knew it was loaded. It was time to finish my job, get Markle behind bars and get the fuck out of Montana. The place only brought me heartache after heartache.

ROB

WHAT THE FUCK was I going to do? In the past eighteen years as alpha, I'd never come across such a fucking mess. I was used to working out problems for other people. Handling disputes. Leading mating ceremonies. Funerals. But this?

It was all about me.

I stood stiff and still as the she-wolf was brought to me for introductions. My pack wanted to match me to this alpha's daughter. I'd balked at the idea because Natalie was to be mine.

But what in the fuck did it matter?

Natalie wasn't Natalie. The whole thing had been a lie.

I didn't have a mate.

And my pack needed me to take one.

Maybe they were right. Maybe I had no fucking sense of what a mate was. That had been proven, loud and clear, when Boyd had helped suss out the truth. How long would she have faked it with me?

Unlike Willow, this pack princess was a shifter. She would ease the minds of assholes like Nathan as well as elders who'd stood beside me all these years. Tom and Janet wouldn't bring someone untrustworthy. They wouldn't bring a liar, like Willow. I trusted their judgement just as they'd trusted mine all this time.

The sooner I forgot about the fake Natalie Shefield the better. My wolf was angry, but not with me this time. He'd been betrayed, too. He'd mark the pack princess because she was our last chance. There were no other options. That was all we'd ever get out of life.

Happiness wasn't in the books for me, but if I mated her, at least I wouldn't die of moon madness. Hopefully.

"Well," I said. I couldn't think of anything else to say. It seemed I'd turned to stone. Completely dead.

Boyd took over for me. "We're having a barbecue," he said to the newcomers. "Why don't you come on back?"

Tom and Janet appeared out of nowhere, tentative smiles on their faces.

"We were thinking you and Kara could head up to the lodgehouse on the mountain. Show her the hunting grounds and have some private time together," Janet said.

Jesus fucking Christ. They wanted me to take her up there and fuck her.

Mark her youthful flesh with my teeth. First thing.

The idea turned my stomach, but my knees had been knocked out from under me by Willow.

Fucking Willow who wasn't Natalie. The human who tricked me to use for her investigation.

"Fine," I muttered, pulling the keys out of my pocket for the truck. I tipped my head at her. "Let's go."

Her eyes were big, face pale. The poor girl didn't want this any more than I did, and I wasn't being all that nice. That wasn't fair to her, so I took a deep breath, let it out, to calm myself. Of course, that meant I picked up her scent.

Sweet. Gentle. It did nothing for my wolf.

I opened the passenger door for her and helped her

climb in, even though she was perfectly capable of doing so herself.

I started the truck and drove up the mountain, happy to leave the fucking festivities behind.

It took me a while before I noticed the tension in the cab. The awkward silence.

Now we were alone together, driving further up into the hills, for the two of us to "get to know each other."

I couldn't blame Kara. She sat beside me, ankles crossed, shoulders back. A small smile played at her lips, but I could tell it was forced. She was tense, and if I felt like I was being set up, then she must feel like she was being sold off.

"I'm sorry," I said, looking over from my seat as we bumped along down the dirt road.

She looked up at me through her dark lashes. I had to admit, she was beautiful. Strong. Well-built. Dark haired, full curves, a sweet scent. My wolf couldn't find anything truly unappealing about her.

"I'm sorry," she said back and laughed awkwardly.

"Kara—" I began.

"I don't want this," she blurted.

Something in me relaxed. My wolf, maybe.

"I'm twenty-two and know my own mind." Her voice was soft but adamant. "I'm sorry, Alpha, but it's the truth."

The truth. Fuck, the first thing this woman gave me was honesty.

"I don't want this either." The words sounded rough but true. I may not want Willow any longer, but there was no way I could mark another female. It would be impossible.

She relaxed. "You're older." Her tanned skin glowed with embarrassment as she looked away. "I mean, older than me. You're alpha. I think you know your mind, too."

"I do."

"Can't you stop this?"

I pulled over in a turnaround and parked the truck. No way I was taking her up to that cabin like a virgin sacrifice.

"It's stopped," I promised.

"Just like that?" she asked, with almost wonder.

"Just like that," I repeated. Cocking my head, I studied her. "Do you want a mate?"

Her eyes lit up with pleasure. "Oh yes. Very much so." That didn't bode well. "But not you," she added. "With all due respect, Alpha—"

"Rob, please. If a couple of elders think they can sequester us until our wolves have decided we're to be mates, then you should at least call me by my name."

She studied me for a minute, bit her lip. "Can I tell you the truth?"

I sighed. "Please." My mind immediately went to Natalie. To Willow. To her lies. Truth seemed to be a good thing right about now.

"I know who my mate is... and it's not you."

I almost laughed—relief my only response. "You've found your mate?"

I was fourteen years older, and I'd finally thought I'd found mine. Too bad she wasn't worthy.

"Yes. He's in the Wind Rivers pack. We met in January at the winter games. I told my father, but Callum's not an alpha. He's an artist. A glass blower and makes the most beautiful pieces." Her hand went to a glass pendant attached to a chain about her neck.

I didn't like the idea of a father forcing his daughter into an unhappy mating, even if it was because he thought it was best for her. "I can speak to your father."

She quickly shook her head, her long hair sliding across her shoulders. "No, that's all right. He knows how I feel but says I'm too young to know my own mind."

"And I'm too old to find my own mate," I added.

"You should be able to choose."

"I thought I had," I admitted before I caught myself.

She grinned then. "Ooooh. Tell me about her."

I didn't say anything.

"You're a nice guy, Rob. I think we could be friends, right? Tell me about her. I told you about Callum."

I set my elbows on the steering wheel and looked out the windshield, unseeing. "My wolf found our mate, but she's human."

I left out the part that she'd fooled me, that she was a liar. That wasn't part of this. It was about the wolf's connection to another.

"Human," she replied, surprised.

I blew out my breath. "Yeah, you can see why that's a problem. If your dad wants you matched to an alpha, you can see that my pack wants me to be matched to another wolf."

"You don't want me then," she said, without the least bit of upset in her voice.

I shook my head. "And you don't want me."

"You know what we should do?" she asked. "We go out there and tell everyone we found our mates."

I couldn't help but laugh. "That's going to go over like a lead balloon."

"So? Don't you want to be happy?"

Happiness.

Happiness was out of fucking reach for me. Fate made sure of that when she paired me with a lying human. "I'm alpha," I said more sternly than I meant to. "My needs and happiness come second to my pack."

"That's not fair," she countered.

I started the truck and turned it around to head back. "One thing you'll learn with age is that life sure as fuck isn't fair. Where's your mate now?"

If I couldn't have my mate, it didn't mean Kara couldn't be happy with hers.

"On his pack land."

"I'll summon him here and arrange the mating myself. As alpha, I can see it done."

Her mouth fell open, and I remembered when Natalie had done the same thing. All I'd thought about at the time was what my dick would look like with those full lips around it. With Kara, I thought nothing of the sort.

"Really?"

I reached over and gave her hand a squeeze. "You found your mate. Nothing should keep you apart."

I let go, then rubbed the ache in my chest. My words rang true for everyone...but me.

I wouldn't have Kara, although she seemed to be a strong, kind, smart woman. She'd make an excellent alpha mate, but she didn't belong to me. And honestly, I wouldn't have her.

My wolf wanted Nat—Willow—even though I'd known all along I couldn't have her. Her duplicity was the perfect excuse I needed to steer clear. She'd do her job and go home, wherever the fuck that was.

I'd had fun. My wolf had had some fun times. Enough to carry us over until the moon madness finished us. I'd just ensure the alpha line was secure before that happened.

24

WILLOW

I MARCHED to the end of the Shefield property and split the barbed wire to step between it.

Rob and I had repaired the fence where the bull came through, but I had yet to confront Markle about it. I'd been saving it as an excuse to be on his property at some point. And truthfully? I'd been too wrapped up in spending time with Rob for the last week to use that excuse.

Now? It was time.

I'd wasted a week, but now I was back on the job.

Except the time hadn't been wasted. It had been everything I needed to live. Now it was all gone. Returning to the life I had before Rob felt like jumping in a lake with cement shoes on.

Nothing could be done about that.

I'd hurt him. He wasn't going to forgive me. Even if he

did, I couldn't stay. I had a job back in Phoenix. Or wherever I went on assignment next.

Except that thought made the brick in the pit of my stomach sink even deeper.

I walked toward Markle's barn and stable, keeping a wary eye out for that damn bull, in case Markle had moved it again. I couldn't decide if he'd put it on my property to scare me or as revenge for dating Rob.

I saw the young ranch hand come out of the stable. Jack, if I remembered correctly.

"Hi!" I made my voice bright and friendly and waved with a smile when he looked over.

God, I used to love playing this part—the sexy girl next door asking for a cup of sugar. This time, it turned my stomach.

I didn't want to live a lie any more.

I didn't want to do it ever again.

Which meant... my life had been completely blown to smithereens.

"Hi!" The young ranch hand walked over and tipped his hat. "Mr. Markle isn't around right now."

"Oh, okay. Maybe you can help me. The other day, I found his bull on my property."

The young man's eyes widened. "Oh no."

"Yeah, it scared the bejeezus out of me. Lucky for me it wandered back, but I was wondering if you knew how it got over to my side of the fence?" I laughed gently. "I mean, it didn't fly over."

Jack took his hat off and scratched his head. "No ma'am, I don't. I'm sorry. I will check all the fences right away."

"Thanks, I would appreciate that." I played dumb. "What's the bull for, anyway? Are you going to sell him?"

"No, he's here for breeding. We just sell a few cows off every so often."

"Oh yeah?" I twirled a lock of hair around my finger and sat into one hip. "Just a few?"

His eyes tracked my movements.

"I know, it's strange if you ask me. Seems like it'd make more sense to sell them all at once. Maybe he don't want to buy another trailer. Not the way I'd do it, but it's not my ranch." He shrugged.

"Well, I'd love to watch you load them up. The cows, I mean. I've never seen a working ranch before."

A grin creased his youthful face. "Well, I don't load them. I just bring 'em down into the chute. Mr. Markle likes to load them himself after sundown and transport at night, so it's not too hot and uncomfortable for the cattle."

Uh huh. Sure. The only way Markle probably liked a cow was medium rare.

"Well, that's very humane of him. When will that be? I'd love to watch that part."

His grin broadened like he thought I was cute. "Well, sure. I'm bringin' "em down tomorrow evening. You're welcome to come down."

"It wouldn't be too much of a bother if I came back to watch? I'll stay out of the way, I promise."

Jack's gaze darted toward Markle's house, like he was suddenly unsure. I wasn't surprised considering what an asshole Markle was. "Uh, yeah. I think that would be fine. I mean, it's fine with me. I don't think Mr. Markle would care."

"Well, I'll ask him when I come," I said sweetly. "Thanks."

I turned and headed back toward my place.

Perfect. If Markle followed routine, which most drug

runners did once they found a method that worked, he'd load the drugs in after the cows, like I saw last time. If I could get down there and check out the crates before they were loaded, I'd have everything I needed to take Markle down.

And Jack just gave me an excuse for being there if I got caught.

I walked back to the house, trying to keep my gaze from lifting toward Wolf Ranch.

Trying to ignore the stab of pain in my chest that seemed like it would never go away. I ached for Rob. For the life he had here, the family. For his dick. And his heart.

Focus on the job, Willow.

It was the only thing I had left.

25

ROB

THE SHAKING of my bed made me groan.

"Get up, asshole."

"What the fuck?" I growled.

"You've had two days."

Colton.

"I've never known you to drink yourself into a fucking stupor."

Boyd.

I blinked, tried not to have sharp spikes drill into my skull as I did so. My bed was soft. Warm. I didn't want to move. I was pretty sure I'd been in it for twenty-four hours straight.

"I'm keeping away the moon madness," I muttered. "And thoughts about Natalie. I mean, Willow. Whatever the fuck her name is."

One of them kicked the bed.

My stomach flip flopped.

"You smell like the floor at Cody's after closing." Again, Colton.

"Are you still wearing the same clothes as at the picnic?" Fucking Boyd.

Groaning, I sat up facing the window. It was dark out. Definitely not time for them to be getting me out of bed. My foot kicked a whiskey bottle across the floor.

"Fuck off."

My mouth tasted like something died, and I wasn't sure if my head was going to stay attached to my body. After I'd called Kara's mate's pack and requested the guy's presence here on Wolf land, I'd led her back to her dad and Tom and Janet. They'd left soon after, and I was sure she'd told them the plan for her mating by now.

I'd still do the mating ceremony if they wanted, but it wasn't required for a true match.

After they left, I found the whiskey and drowned myself in it. My wolf had pushed me to go after Willow, but I refused to do it. The only way to get my wolf to stop and for me to forget was to get stumbling drunk.

"We did. For two days. Take a shower and get yourself together," Colton said. "You need to eat some food."

Two days. I'd accomplished my goal. But why they were having me surface now, I had no idea.

"Why?" I ran a hand through my hair absently, then over my jaw.

"We're not talking to you like this. Shower. Shave that fucking beard," Boyd ordered. "We've got some steaks on the grill."

"Don't boss me around. I'm the fucking alpha around here."

"Oh yeah?" Colton asked, whacking me on the back of my head, making me groan. "Then act like it."

"We give you ten minutes then we're coming in after you," Boyd said. "The last thing I want to do is see your junk, so you better fucking move."

Fifteen minutes later—I refused to bow down to my younger brother—I grabbed a glass from the kitchen cabinet and filled it with water. I drank it in one long gulp. Only then did I turn and face my brothers. And Clint.

"Fuck," I whispered.

Clint tossed a bottle of ibuprofen at me. I caught it with my free hand, then set my water down to get the lid open and take some. The shower had helped. I felt a little better with fresh clothes and the itchy start of a beard gone. My head still throbbed, and my stomach felt like it was made of battery acid. I couldn't remember the last thing I ate.

"You did a good thing with Kara and her mate," Clint said. He sat at the kitchen table, hands folded on the scarred surface. A plate piled with steak sat in the middle of the table, but it only made my stomach turn.

Colton must've understood because he went to the bread box and pulled out a roll. "Eat this."

It had to be one of Marina's since it had a golden exterior and a fancy twist in it, but it was plain. Thank fuck.

I gnawed off a chunk and chewed, hoping it would stay down. Shifters shouldn't get hung over. I didn't know what the fuck was wrong with me.

Oh yes, I did. I'd been drinking non-stop to keep from going after Willow and even a shifter's metabolism and ability to heal couldn't compete with constant guzzling of alcohol.

"He showed up yesterday. Kara's mate," Colton said. "Needless to say, they were mated by dark."

I grunted in reply. So fucking easy. Literally. Kara had her mate's mark on her neck, and here I was, nursing a wicked hangover with my brothers and Clint.

"You trying to get me to drink some more?" I asked them.

"No, fucker. You need to go get your mate."

I eyed Boyd. "You mean the human I can't have, or do you mean the undercover DEA agent posing as our neighbor?"

Clint shook his head. "Your mate. The one your wolf wants."

"He doesn't know what he wants," I grumbled.

"Oh yeah?" Colton asked. "She's been at Markle's place a couple times now."

I tossed my glass into the empty fireplace, shattering it into pieces. "Are you fucking kidding me?"

The men didn't even blink by my action.

"Yeah, just as I thought," Colton said. "She's yours."

"If she's mine, why the fuck's she with Markle? Did he take her wine this time?" I sounded like a petty, snarly wolf pup. I couldn't help it. I felt like I should just shoot myself and the idea of Markle anywhere near Natalie made me want to rip the asshole's throat out.

"Did she tell you who she suspected of drug running?"

I shook my head, realized that was a bad move, then grabbed a new glass from the cabinet for more water.

"I told her it wasn't us."

Boyd laughed. "For an alpha, you're pretty fucking stupid." I just stared at him. "Did it ever occur to you it might be Markle?"

I stopped, glass halfway to my mouth, and stared at him. "Markle?"

"Why the fuck do you think she went over there with

wine that night?" Colton asked. "Why the DEA had her posing as Natalie Shefield, Markle's *next door neighbor.*"

Markle. A drug runner. That actually made a lot of sense.

"We've been watching her," Clint said evenly. "Since she left the other day from the picnic."

My gaze narrowed and homed in on my oldest friend. "Why?"

He sighed. "Because she's your mate, and if you're not going to watch out for her, someone had to."

"She's fucking DEA, you asshole," Boyd said. "Undercover. She's here for a reason, and it's not to ride your dick. I suppose that was a surprise twist for her, too."

"I'm sure she can take care of herself," Colton began. "But she's not here to turn the house into a fucking bed and breakfast. She's dealing with real bad shit. She needs backup, and I don't see any from the DEA."

"She's doing her job, brother," Boyd said, his voice calmer than usual. "Do you really think she wanted to keep herself a secret? To lie? Do you take her for someone like that? You've got a job, too, you moron. Being alpha, you have to make sacrifices, too. You're more alike than you think."

I sighed, even though what he said made sense. "That still doesn't make her my mate."

"No, your wolf made her your mate."

"She's *human!*" I growled, the windows shaking. "The pack won't allow it."

Colton came over and stood right before me. "You're alpha. Tell the pack to get in line, or they can walk. You're going to *die,* brother, if you don't mate her."

"I'm not mating her to save my life."

"Why the fuck not? We all do. That's the point!" Boyd shouted.

"Do you want her?" Clint asked, quieter than either Boyd or Colton.

Did I want her? Images of her flooded my brain. Fucking herself with the dildo. Pointing a gun at my chest—both times. Her bright smile. The tears that ran down her face when she confessed her lie.

"Yes," I admitted. "Fuck, yes."

"Then get her. Who gives a shit about Nathan and the others? We're better off with him out of the pack. If your wolf says you have a human mate, then that's the way it is."

"What about pups? They won't be able to shift." I glanced at Boyd because Audrey was going to have a half-human, half-shifter pup in a few months. Who probably couldn't shift.

"What about an asteroid hitting the planet? You can't plan for everything, just like you never expected to find your mate next door."

Were they right? Was I being a dumbass? My wolf thought so. Now that I was sober, or on the way to getting there, it was pushing me to go after Natalie. Willow. To make her mine. To grovel until she forgave me. Until she let me bite her and make her mine.

Human or not.

"I'm going," I said. The moment I decided, my wolf perked up. Energy returned to my body, and the hangover instantly faded.

I stepped out the front door, only to find three cars pulling in our drive. "Aw, fuck."

Boyd, Colton and Clint followed me out to see what had made me curse and added a few of their own.

It was Nathan Brown and his Madison Range kin, along with a half dozen of my pack's elders.

I stood on the porch and waited. I was still their fucking

alpha, even if they did want to commit mutiny. Colton, Boyd and Clint flanked me.

Art Grayback, one of the pack elders who cozied up with Nathan, stalked toward me, looking angry. "You mated the she-wolf intended for you to another male."

I nodded. "She made her choice," I said calmly. "And she didn't choose me."

Art crossed his arms over his chest. "Who did you choose then?"

I looked back at him evenly. Yeah, I had a fuck-ton of problems, but I was still alpha. I couldn't show weakness of any kind. "I haven't mated yet."

"Rumor has it you're interested in that new neighbor of yours. A *human.*" He sneered, as if *human* was a bad word.

If it were the new moon, I might've been able to keep my cool. But we were approaching full, which meant my temper —especially when it came to my mate—ran hot. I stalked down the steps and grabbed a fistful of his shirt. "That's right. My wolf has chosen a human for a mate. Do you have something to say about it?"

Art paled and tried to push free. "Now listen here—"

"No. I'm done listening. I've listened. I've considered. I've made my choice. The human is mine. If you want to defect to the Madison Range pack and be with the others, be my guest. My brothers and I will be staying here in Cooper Valley. With or without the rest of you." I released him, giving him a shove backward. "Make your choice." I gave every male there my fiercest stare. "Right now. And know, all of you—if you walk away today, you're not coming back."

Nathan gave a mirthless laugh. "You just killed our pack, Rob Wolf. Now there won't be anyone to carry your line to the next generation. No alpha to lead. Whether the pack members leave now or in twenty years makes no difference.

The pack dies with you." He spit on the ground. "What a fucking waste."

One by one, the wolves got back in their cars and drove away.

I didn't fucking care.

Fate sent me a human. That was who I was claiming.

If she'd have me.

I started jogging down the path toward her house. I need to fix things between us. And it couldn't wait another fucking minute.

26

WILLOW

I WATCHED Markle's place from the master bedroom window all evening. His fancy pickup truck had been gone all afternoon. My guess was he'd gone to pick up the drugs from wherever Murrieta dropped them. I didn't take Markle for the kind of guy to go pick up drugs. It was beneath a billionaire to get his hands dirty. But he was the minion now. Murrieta's mule. Literally. Unfortunately, we didn't know about that angle of the operation, but if we got Markle in cuffs and in an interrogation room, we'd be able to get the details. Especially if we had him with the drugs. To Murrieta, Markle was a little fish. As for Markle, he only cared about himself, and if he could finagle any kind of deal with the DEA, I figured he'd squeal like a pig.

I kicked myself for not seeing him leave, so I could tail him, but so long as I got him with the drugs now, we were in business.

It was eleven o'clock when I heard the crunch of tires over gravel and saw his truck pull in. Tucking my gun in a holster at my back, I pulled a lightweight jacket on over the top to hide it.

I called Vaughn. "He's back, I'm going down to get it all on film."

"Only photos," he ordered. "Do not try to make an arrest on your own. You might be in Bumfuck, Montana, but bad shit still happens. You call for backup before you do anything, understand?"

"Yes, sir."

He hung up.

I rechecked my weapon out of habit and re-holstered it behind my back.

It was showtime.

Outside, the moon shone high in the sky, lighting my path. It made it harder to blend in. I hadn't dressed in black or put smudges on my face this time since I had the excuse that I'd been invited to watch the cattle load-up, but I still would have preferred not to be seen. If I could somehow get to the feed bags and open them to verify they contained drugs, then I'd have everything I needed. I could take pictures with my phone and instantly send them back to Vaughn. That would ensure a search warrant.

I stopped when I got close and used the night vision camera to see what was going on. Jack was loading cattle into the small pen beside the chute like he'd said he would. The cows would walk up and onto the hauler, perhaps with a little coaxing for the first one. The rest would follow. The truck hadn't arrived yet, but if they were being herded together, it was coming soon. Markle had backed his pickup up to the barn which meant that was where I needed to be.

I stayed low and crept closer, skirting around the outside

of the barn and hiding behind it. I waited until I heard the slam of a door and the pickup start. Then Markle pulled away, stopping to tell Jack to go home and he'd get the cattle loaded when the trailer showed up.

To me, it meant he was going to add the drugs. No way would he load cattle all on his own otherwise.

I touched the gun at my back for reassurance before I slid in the shadows along the side of the barn. Jack started a beat up twenty-year-old pickup and pulled out, his tail lights receding down the drive. Meanwhile, Markle was parking his vehicle in front of his house, hopefully going inside to wait. I darted around the corner and slipped into the open door of the barn.

It definitely wasn't an animal barn. Or at least it wasn't currently being used for them. There was no tang of manure. No hay. Along the front wall was a stack of crates. Nothing huge but could definitely fit in the back of a pickup. I tried to open one, but it was nailed shut.

Dammit.

I pulled out my hunting knife to use to pry the lid off. It took some work, but I finally got it loose. I quietly propped the lid against the crate and peered inside. It looked like a plastic bag full of cattle feed. I sliced it open with my knife and fished around inside.

Bingo! I pulled out a package of snowy white powder. Cocaine.

I couldn't help the grin. After months of investigation, one awful date and a goodnight kiss, I had Markle. All I needed now was to get some pics off to Vaughn for that backup and—

A gun cocked right beside my ear. "Put it down and turn around, real slow."

Fuck!

Markle.

How had I not heard him? My senses were usually so sharp.

I moved slowly, lowering the cocaine to the crate then lifting my hands in the air and turning around.

"Most women give me a BJ for a dinner date. When you didn't put out, or at least drop to your knees, I had to wonder. Who the fuck are you?" he demanded. His usual swagger was replaced with fierce determination. Darkness. Evil.

I pursed my lips. Did I bluff or throw my badge in his face? Neither seemed like a great option at the moment, not with his pistol pointed right at me.

"Murrieta sent me. To watch over you. Make sure you didn't skim any from him."

His eyes narrowed. I could tell he wasn't sure because it was probably something the kingpin might have done, but the fact that he didn't look confused told me I was right about his connection with the cartel.

"You're lying." He shifted from foot to foot, his eyes darting around the barn and out the door, like he was looking for my back up.

My non-existent back up.

Shit! If only I'd had time to call for help. No one knew I was here. Vaughn was probably tucked in his bed sleeping.

"Nice try, but that bastard Murrieta doesn't send women to do a man's job. No fucking way. He keeps his women tied up and on their knees. So, who are you? FBI? DEA?"

Okay, he didn't love Murrieta. I could use that to my advantage.

"How did he get you into this?" I asked, feigning sympathy. "What's he got on you?" I really wished I had a recording device on me, in case I got anything out of him that could be used in court. It would still be great to hear the whole plan from the horse's mouth. While I had him with the drugs, the puzzle wasn't complete.

"Let's just say he didn't understand the concept of risk in his investments."

"When you were in New York you invested his money in a hedge fund and lost it," I said, thinking aloud. Now the connection between the two men made more sense. "He holds you responsible."

"Shut up!" he snapped, the gun wavering. "Get down on your knees. Keep your hands in the air. What agency are you from?"

"DEA," I said to mollify him. He wasn't a bad guy like Murrieta, only caught up and used as one of his many pawns. Sure, he was a dick and deserved to be behind bars, but he was a low-level thug and had little experience with this aspect of drug running. He was starting to lose it, and I didn't want to get my head shot off because he panicked. I slowly lowered to my knees, hands in the air. I just needed a momentary distraction—time enough to reach for the gun at my back.

"Where's your partner?"

I thought quickly. Should I pretend to have a partner? I wasn't sure if it would buy me time either way, but I answered, "Searching your house."

He spared a quick glance toward the open barn door, but it wasn't long enough for me to reach for my gun. I had to keep him talking until that moment came.

"So, Murrieta has you running drugs for him," I said, stalling. "Did he buy you this ranch? Or was this your idea? I bet you don't even like Montana."

"Shut up!" Markle shouted, stepping toward me. He held the gun right to my temple. "Shut the hell up."

"I'm impressed. You've had even the DEA stumped. How are you doing it?" I wanted to play into his vanity, to his need for power.

"Cattle trailer." His ego's too big not to tell.

"Cattle trailer to Canada? Smart. Some way to get narcotics over the border. Where's the holding location? I looked at the stack of crates beside me. Not here."

HIs eyes narrowed. "How'd you connect me with him? What tipped you off?"

We were both trying to get information out of each other before he pulled that trigger.

"We traced a payment from his off-shore account to yours before you bought the place." I fed him a bone. "So, you keep the shipments light and frequent to avoid suspicion. Selling just a few head of cows to Canada every other week."

Markle pursed his lips, eyes narrowed.

I kept talking. "Why do you want the Shefield land so much?" I wondered. That was one thing I never understood. Why make trouble if he didn't want to bring attention to himself?

"Murrieta wants a runway."

Ah. The land was big enough for that, especially if he took down the fence at the property line. It would work for small planes to move drugs easily. They flew low and stayed off the radar.

He cocked the gun. "Enough talking."

"You don't want to kill me," I said, my voice sounding more stable than I expected, even though my heart was beating double time and sweat dripped down my back. "You definitely don't want to add a murder charge to trafficking of narcotics."

"Oh, I'm not going to kill you. You're right. I don't need

that kind of rap. I'm going to give you to Murrieta for his flesh trade. He has a special affinity for white women. Especially those he feels have crossed him. Torture is his specialty." Markle gazed down at me with cruelty in his expression. Issuing threats had calmed him, though. The gun was steady now in his hand. He'd regained his footing.

That meant I was in big trouble.

27

ROB

I KNEW IMMEDIATELY NATALIE—WILLOW—WASN'T in the house. I would've heard her breathing. Hell, even her pulse. Now that I'd made the choice that she was to be mine... officially, my wolf was attuned to her. Or the lack of her.

Her scent was in the air around the exterior of the house but not strong. There was a distinct path of the scent. She rarely used the front door. My wolf picked her up going in and out of the back door more. I followed across the back porch and back down the steps, across the grass and toward—

"Fuck," I said, cutting through the night. She was at Markle's.

I knew it. My wolf knew it. It was after eleven. Unless she was at his place to fuck, she was there for work. I didn't even give the first any thought. I'd satisfied her. She didn't need Markle for that. Besides, now that I could see past my anger at her secrets, I knew she would never cheat. She'd been just as invested in *us* as I'd been.

No. She was over at Markle's because of her fucking job. Which meant she was all alone. The DEA didn't send someone undercover unless they had just cause. That meant they had something on Markle. Something big enough that warranted constant surveillance. Even having someone pose as a friendly next-door neighbor and offer wine in order to get intel.

It was easy to follow her path. A human could have followed the knocked down grass in the moonlight, but my wolf followed her scent. Strong and leading me right to her. Right to Markle's fancy new barn.

My wolf hearing picked up the voices even before I could see inside. The air was still, and I couldn't miss their words.

"You don't want to kill me," Willow said. "You definitely don't want to add a murder charge to trafficking of narcotics."

Oh shit. Markle had found her. Or knew she wasn't just a hot neighbor.

"Oh, I'm not going to kill you," Markle countered. "You're right. I don't need that kind of rap. I'm going to give you to Murrieta for his flesh trade. He has a special affinity for white women. Especially those he feels have crossed him. Torture is his specialty."

My wolf snarled. I saw red. It took all my will to keep from shifting right there. My mate was being threatened. Not just threatened, worse. But I needed to keep my head because Markle had a gun, and my mate wouldn't survive a bullet.

I had no fucking idea who Murrieta was, but the words *flesh trade* and *torture* stood out. I'd thought Markle was an asshole neighbor for putting his cattle on the Shefield land.

I'd been blind to how evil he really was. Willow wanted to bring him down. Hell, the federal government did.

Now I did, too. There was no fucking way he was going to be breathing much longer.

I went to the barn door, staying in the shadows to peer inside. Willow was on her knees, Markle standing above her with a gun to her head. My wolf shoved to the surface again, trying to take control. He needed to save her, but I shoved him back down. The gun held me back from tearing out his throat with my fangs. If I startled him, he could shoot her in a second.

I had to redirect him away from her. I was a wolf. He could shoot me full of holes like Swiss cheese, and I'd heal. I looked around on the ground, found a small rock. I tossed it into the barn but lobbed it hard so that it hit well past them.

The thunk was loud when it hit the floor, both Markle and Willow whipping their heads toward the sound, their gazes away from me. Willow took the opportunity to push Markle's gun to the side and hop to her feet. With both her hands, she gripped his wrist to keep the gun pointing away from her.

I ran into the barn to help, but Markle had strength and fury on his side. He bent his elbow and with his free arm, grabbed Willow by the back of her neck, yanking her toward him.

The gun went off before I made it halfway to them. I saw her wide eyes, the way her shoulders slumped and knew she'd been hit. Markle released her, and she fell to the ground.

I howled, my wolf taking over. I got to Markle and grabbed him, ready to rip his head from his body. Out of the corner of my eye, I saw Willow lean to the side and grab her gun which she had at her back.

She raised it and fired, point blank at the center of Markle's forehead. Bullseye. The shot had gotten within a foot of me, but I hadn't been afraid she'd hit me. Sure, there had been no time to react, but there was no better shot than my mate. Like he had with Willow, I let Markle fall to the floor. There was no question he was dead. The back half of his head was missing.

I didn't give Markle another look but dropped to my knees next to Willow, looked her over. Assessed.

"Fuck," I croaked. Blood quickly spread across her torso. I lifted the bottom of her shirt, saw the entry wound.

She whimpered and her body shook. Shock. Fear.

"Willow, no" I breathed. Fear cut through me like never before. We were twenty miles from town. Twenty miles from the hospital, and she'd been shot in the gut.

I leaned over her, looked down into her face. Sweat dotted her brow, the color quickly leaching from her face.

"Hang on. Don't you fucking die on me now," I swore.

She panted, her hand coming to her wound to cover it. She hissed. "It hurts. Fuck."

I grabbed my phone. Dialed. My fingers were shaking so bad I almost dropped the phone as I lifted it to my ear. "Boyd. Willow's been shot. Bad. Bring Audrey to Markle's barn. *Now!*"

I dropped the phone to the dirt and shucked my shirt, pressed it over her wound to stanch the blood flow.

"I'm sorry," she whispered, then winced. Her eyes were filled with pain. Regret. Fear. "I'm sorry. It wasn't a lie."

"Shh, angel. I know."

"How I feel about you wasn't a lie."

I leaned over her again, so she could only see me.

"Angel, you were doing your job. I know that. You did nothing wrong. I'm to blame. I shouldn't have doubted you or pushed you away. It doesn't change what I knew the first second I caught your scent—you're mine. My mate. My heart. I love you. Now *fight.*"

Determination filled her eyes, but she moaned in pain. She pulled out her phone with shaking hands. "Call... Vaughn. My boss. Tell him..."

"Okay, I'll call him. You just hang in there, angel."

She was going to die. I knew it. There was no way I could save her. Audrey was a doctor and could help, but she wouldn't be here for at least five more minutes. Then, we still had to drive to the hospital.

"I love you, Willow. You stay with me. *Stay with me,*" I said. I repeated it over and over as I held her gaze.

Then my wolf instincts prickled. Willow's eye color changed from green to gold.

All at once, she moaned. Loud. Deep.

I stopped breathing.

Her joints cracked and snapped, her clothing ripped. From one blink to the next, Willow shifted from red-haired human to a ginger wolf.

My wolf did a double backflip of joy. Of relief.

Holy. Fucking. Shit.

My mate was a shifter! Which meant she wasn't going to die.

28

ROB

WILLOW STRUGGLED, rolling to her side, then emitting a yip of pain. She was panicking, her amber eyes wild and almost feral. This hadn't been one of her secrets. I was sure of it. She hadn't known she was a wolf—or part wolf—because she sure as hell had smelled like a human before.

Which meant... she'd never shifted before and only did so now because of the pain of being shot. Her biology kicked in to save her life. No one had seen her like this before. No one knew how perfect she was... human or wolf.

I stroked my hand over her soft fur. "Shh... settle." I put alpha command in my voice. "It's all right. There's nothing to be afraid of. You're a shifter, like me. That's why my wolf chose you." I smiled down at her. "I know you hurt, but shifting is a good thing. You'll heal and quickly. Your body knows what to do. Don't be afraid, you're going to be just fine."

My words must have penetrated because she stilled. I felt the frantic beat of her wolf heart beneath my palm, the silkiness of her fur. I saw the gunshot wound, staining her cinnamon fur a fierce red. The blood wasn't pumping from her now but slowed to a trickle.

That eased my own wolf. "That's it. Just relax. Let your wolf heal."

I looked into her eyes, just as I had a few moments before and tried to comfort her. "You're so beautiful as a wolf. Didn't know you had it in you, huh?" I smiled.

Finally, I was at peace. She wasn't going to die, but she needed to be talked through the healing process, the shift back to human form. If she'd never done it before, she wouldn't know how.

My parents had talked about our first shift for years. I never remembered a time when we hadn't talked about it. What it would feel like. What I'd do when I shifted. How I shifted back. If a first shift came early, there was some danger that a teen wolf couldn't shift back. Sometimes it took an alpha command to make it happen. I'd been called in a few times to help new wolves who got stuck.

I remembered what Willow had told me about being in foster care as a child. That part was probably the truth. She'd given me the truths she could. Maybe she hadn't known one or both of her parents at all—that's why she hadn't known she was a shifter.

I wondered if she'd had any hints of wolf, if she'd had any clues to it. Signs she wouldn't have known were the need of her inner wolf to be revealed.

"Holy shit."

I looked up when Boyd and Audrey came rushing in but skidded to a stop as they stared down at us. Audrey had her assessing gaze on Markle for about two seconds, then to us.

Dead was dead. No matter how skilled a doctor Audrey was, she wasn't fixing Markle.

"Um... Rob," Boyd said. "Is that—"

"Willow's a shifter."

He grinned. "No shit."

No shit.

"Did you know?" Audrey asked, squatting down beside me. From what she and Boyd told me, she'd seen James get shot by Markle and shift, and she'd watched him heal so she knew what was going to happen. There really wasn't anything for her to do to help.

"Had no fucking idea," I said, continuing to stroke Willow's body, pet her head, rub an ear, her belly. Stroking all of her to let her know I was here, that it was okay. "The pain from being shot must have triggered it."

"The wound's already closing up," Boyd commented.

I looked down, saw that it was no longer bleeding.

"I'll help her shift back." I looked down at Willow on the ground. "Right, angel? I'll help you when it's time. You heal faster in wolf form, though, so we'll give it a little longer. Then you can call your boss, and we'll get this mess here sorted out."

"Got a blanket in your truck?" I asked Boyd. Willow's clothes were in bloody tatters beneath her. The last thing I wanted was for her to feel self-conscious after she shifted back... naked.

"I'll get it," Audrey offered, starting to stand.

Boyd set a hand on her shoulder, keeping her from getting to her feet. "No. You stay here. I'll get it."

"I'm not an expert on shifter healing, but she'll be fine, right?" Audrey looked to me.

I nodded. "Yes. I'd say... oh, there it is." The bullet was starting to emerge from the wound, and she whimpered. If I wasn't used to seeing this kind of healing, it would have been weird the way a wolf's body expelled foreign objects.

Willow whimpered but went silent as the bullet slid from her and onto the packed dirt floor.

Boyd returned, and I took the blanket from him. "Come on, darlin'," he said to Audrey. He held out his hand, and she took it, rising. "Let's give them a little privacy. We'll go get some clothes for her. Let us know how she wants to play this. Audrey can be her doctor if she needs to go to the hospital. She's used to fake injuries." He gave Audrey a wink.

They walked off as I checked Willow's wound. It wasn't fully healed, but she could shift back now.

"All right, angel. It's time. I know you're scared 'cause this is all new, but we shifters do this all the time. You'll just have to catch up. To shift back, you need to close your eyes and think. Think about your human body. How you stand on two feet. Your gorgeous red locks." I grinned. "Even between your luscious thighs. Think human, and you'll just shift."

I continued to stroke her as she stared at me. Blinked.

"Close your eyes now. That's it. It's no big deal. Relax and just let it happen."

She finally closed her eyes, and I waited. I remembered my first shift, how weird it had been. Scary, too. Once I was back in human form and knew I couldn't be stuck as a wolf, it came easier. I just had to get her to shift back this once, and I'd be able to guide her through the rest of being a shifter.

"*Shift,*" I commanded, putting an alpha push into the words.

She responded. The familiar sounds happened, and she shifted back. I sighed in relief, a little worried she might not be able to do it. She was probably twice as old as one normally was for a first shift. In fact, I'd never known someone whose first shift came so late.

"There's my angel. Lie still, and the pain will lessen." She sat up slowly, and I pulled her onto my lap, cradling her carefully and wrapping the blanket up around her. "I guess we now know where you're from, huh?"

"Rob... oh my God. That was... I mean, did I just—"

"Turn into a wolf?" I finished for her. "I assume you didn't know."

She shook her head, her hair brushing my bare chest. "I was an orphan. I've been in foster care my whole life. I didn't know anything about my biological parents. But, God, this explains things. My sense of smell was always... far too keen. I prefer the outdoors. My instincts are good. I like to run."

"I like to look at you when you run." I thought of her in those tiny shorts. "I like to run better in wolf form. Now you can go with me."

"It was fate, then wasn't it?" she murmured. "You and I?"

I smiled, cradling her face. "Definitely fate." And that was the honest truth. I wouldn't have cared if she wasn't a shifter, but now we had more to share. More to understand about each other.

"I know who you are, Willow. You're mine. But if you want to find your family, it'll be easier now. We just have to find your home pack. Ginger wolves are rare. It shouldn't be too hard. Although I hope you'll stay here with me. To be my alpha mate."

She studied my face. "Can't argue with fate, can I?" She smiled.

I kissed her—gently—because she was still weak. And we had to deal with a dead body and probably a whole bunch of federal agents. Later, I'd kiss her thoroughly. I'd kiss her all fucking night long.

WILLOW

THE LOCAL SHERIFF and his deputy arrived first. I was still a little lightheaded from the gunshot, or maybe from discovering I was a shifter, but years of protocol pushed to the forefront.

"Agent Johnson?"

"Yes, sir."

After I'd shifted back, I'd called Vaughn and tried to convince him to send backup, so we could catch whoever showed up with the empty trailer for the cows and drugs, but he wouldn't have it—especially after he heard I'd already been shot at. He'd notified the sheriff to get there immediately, and the sheriff had arrived with lights flashing, which probably meant whoever was responsible for driving the drugs across the border would keep right on driving past.

I kept my hand over the wound at my side as I reached out to shake his hand. Boyd and Audrey had brought me a change of clothes, which I'd stained a little with blood from my wound to make it look like a bullet just grazed me.

"I'm Sheriff Duncan." He stared at Markle's fallen body in the dirt, repulsion showing on his face. "Is that your perp?"

"Yes. Jett Markle, owner of this ranch." I pointed to the crates of drugs. "We had a shootout after I found his supply." I attempted a wry grin. "Good thing I'm a better shot than he was."

He looked at my side. "You were hit? Do we need to get you to the hospital?"

"No, it's a flesh wound. The neighbor, Dr. Ames, already patched me up." I nodded at Audrey, who had remained to make sure no one tried to get a look at my rapidly healing bullet hole. She'd covered it with a bandage and was prepared to attest to the fact that I had merely been grazed by a bullet and didn't need to go into the hospital tonight.

She stood near Boyd's pickup with Rob and Boyd, who refused to leave us unprotected.

"Evening Sheriff Duncan," Rob lifted a hand in greeting.

The sheriff nodded at Rob and Boyd. "Evening, gentlemen."

"Did my boss tell you there was a possibility of his friends showing up?" I asked.

The sheriff touched the gun at his side. "He told me. I've got back up on the way. If they come, we'll get them."

Yeah, I wasn't so sure about that.

The op hadn't gone as planned. I'd wanted Markle behind bars, so we could use him to get Murrieta. After what happened, I was happy he was dead. His intentions for me didn't make me feel bad in the slightest.

We had the drugs, knew how they arrived at the ranch and how they left and got to Canada.

With Markle dead, there was no information on getting to Murrieta. Vaughn planned to send a guy to the next planned drug pickup at the closed rest area, but it wasn't going to be Murrieta himself. Only another cog in his huge drug wheel.

I'd pretty much blown the case. We were back to square one because Murietta wouldn't give a shit that Markle was dead. He'd been a mere pawn. He'd have another one by tonight to rebuild the drug path to Canada.

The shipments were stopped for now but wouldn't be for long.

I'd failed, and I had no doubt I was out of a job. For once in my life, I didn't care.

Everything I'd thought about myself had been wrong. My name really wasn't Willow Johnson. I'd always known that. Tonight was the first time there was a real clue to who I was. To *what* I was.

I was a shifter.

A shifter!

And that mattered so much more than this stupid case I'd been fixated on for the past year.

"The DEA will be here in the morning, so if your men could just keep watch, it would be much appreciated. I'd like to get back and clean up and get a couple hours sleep before I have to meet them here to search the place and take care of all the procedures and paperwork."

"You're staying at the Shefield place?"

"That's right," I said.

"Okay, Agent. Let me take your statement and then you can go ahead. We'll stay here to protect the crime scene."

Thank God for small town sheriffs.

I looked over at Rob and gave him a weak smile.

Everything had changed. My whole life had turned upside down, and the one thing I knew that mattered—the only thing—was him.

29

WILLOW

"AND NOW, my little ginger she-wolf, it's time for your punishment." Rob backed me up against the bed, tugging my clothes off as he went.

We were at his pack's mountain lodge in the private bedroom in the back. Rob brought me up so I could practice shifting, but first... he had something else in mind.

I'd spent the past day bogged down in procedures. The sheriff and paramedics with Markle's body had left by dawn, but the DEA had remained all day, searching the property, making an inventory of the drugs and working with Canadian customs to watch for other shipments. Markle's drug channel was shut down.

My body had mostly healed. I still had a mark and felt twinges where the bullet hit me, but that was it. My shifter genes had saved my life.

Everything in my life suddenly made sense. What I'd

told Rob when I'd first shifted back: my sensitive nose, my heightened instincts, my love of running. And what I hadn't told him. Why I'd never felt like I belonged in society. Until I'd come to Cooper Valley and found Rob. I knew from my paperwork my birth mother, who had been just a teenager, had been admitted as a Jane Doe to a hospital in Billings. She'd had me and disappeared from her hospital bed, abandoning me. Whether she was the shifter or my dad was, I couldn't be sure, but for some reason, it changed the story for me.

I'd felt abandoned before. Unwanted.

Now I felt special. My parents—or one of them—had given me a gift. I was half-shifter. Able to turn into a beautiful ginger wolf, according to Rob. And I had a mate. I'd known it since the first second he'd barged into my room and caught me with my dildo.

We still had to discuss our future.

I had to decide if being his mate was what I wanted, although there wasn't all that much of a decision.

"Why punishment? I haven't been bad," I replied, allowing him to slip my panties off, so I stood naked before him.

He arched a brow. "You went to Markle's, a known drug dealer, not once, not twice but multiple times without someone with you. I told you I wanted you to stay away from him. That's being a bad girl."

A shiver of excitement ran through me at the same time as remorse. I'd been doing my job, and he'd just been trying to protect me. I could see how he'd have been afraid. God, if I'd seen someone hold a gun to his head... then shoot him. I wanted to throw up. I so deserved to be spanked or whatever he wanted to make amends. To make him feel better, to know I was safe and whole and under his control.

It was over though, and he needed to get past it as much as me. I'd let him do whatever he needed to feel better because it would heal me, too, and not the gunshot wound.

I wouldn't let him sink into the what if's though. "You'll have to catch me, first," I called out, turning and dashing through the lodge.

He stayed a breath behind me but let me get all the way in before he caught me up around the waist and swung me into the air. He tossed and flipped me, so I landed over his shoulder, then carried me back dropped me onto the large bed.

"On your belly, legs spread." His voice was thick and gravelly with desire.

I grinned up at him. "Make me," I taunted because I loved it when he showed me his strength. I loved that he could overpower me. That his commands made my body instantly respond.

What could be sexier?

He laughed and climbed over me, snatching up my wrists. In a flash, he had me on my belly, my wrists pinned behind my back in one of his large hands. With the other, he smacked my ass.

I shrieked and wriggled although pain had changed for me now that I'd found my inner wolf. I registered the sensation, but it was not nearly so uncomfortable. In fact, I rather welcomed it. I shoved my ass up for more.

He spanked harder, alternating slapping one cheek then the other until my whole ass was warm and tingly. "Never put yourself in a situation like that again. No guns. No bad guys. In fact, no other men at all."

Each thing he said was accompanied by a solid spank until I was sure my butt was a fiery shade of red.

"No guns. No men. Only you," I cried out.

He kept going until he felt reassured of my words or that my ass had been spanked enough that I'd learned my lesson.

Only then did he flip me over. He pointed at me and said, "Don't move."

He went to our bags and pulled something out, but I couldn't see it from where I lay. Moving to stand at the foot of the bed, he tossed the object between my parted legs.

It was the big dildo I'd been using the first time I saw him.

"I want to watch."

I looked at the dildo, then him. He was definitely bigger. And harder. Thicker. Longer. I didn't want the latex in my pussy. I wanted him, and I told him so.

Slowly, he shook his head, his dark gaze narrowed, his lids hooded. "Good girls get their pussy's stuffed with big dick."

Oh my God. The dirty talk.

Grabbing the toy, I gripped the base as I would Rob. Spreading my legs nice and wide, just as they'd been the week before, I set the dildo at my entrance, ran it over my folds, getting it wet. The spanking had gotten me hot and ready, and there would be no trouble working it inside me.

I looked to Rob, standing gloriously naked and watching. He gripped his dick and stroked himself as I pushed the dildo into me. Whimpering, I loved the feel of it, but knew Rob would stretch me more. Would sink deeper. Would pound me as hard as I could handle.

I wanted Rob, but he was only going to come to me when he was ready. So I'd make him that way. Gripping the toy's base, I began to fuck myself with it, lifting and lowering my hips to take it, all the while I watched Rob. He wouldn't be able to miss the wet sounds the toy made as I was so wet.

All at once, he growled, leaned over the bed, pushed my hand out of the way. Carefully, he fucked me once, then again with the dildo, then slipped it free. He held it up, shiny with my arousal.

"One of these days, you'll fuck your pussy with that while I take your ass."

I moaned at the visual.

"But now, I want that pussy." With a quick flick of his wrist on my ankle, he flipped me back onto my belly. Then he moved behind me and nudged my knees wider. "Can I come inside you, Willow?" I loved how hungry he sounded, how much watching me play with myself pushed him to the edge. I also loved my real name coming from his lips. He knew who I was, wanted me. The real me. "I want to take you bare, to have nothing between us from now on."

"Yes." I looked over my shoulder at him and found his eyes glowing. I wondered if mine changed color, too, with the need swirling between us. And what shade?

He dragged my hips up until I stood on my knees, then pushed my torso down, still holding my wrists pinned to my back.

I sighed with pleasure the moment his cock dragged through my juices. Pushed back when he nudged at my entrance. Unlike the dildo, he was warm, hard but pliant... and big. So virile. And all for me.

One thrust, and he was in deep. I groaned, closed my eyes at how he felt stretching me open in ways a toy never would. Every time it was like this, as if he'd always be a tight fit.

"I won't be able to hold back, angel," he said hoarsely. "After watching you fuck yourself. Fuck, that was so hot. You're mine now. Understand?"

"Yes," I gasped because it sounded so right. But then I realized what he was saying.

He held himself still deep inside me. "Will you be my mate? Will you accept my mark, to walk beside me, be my alpha mate?"

This wasn't a proposal. The words were more important than that. I knew what he was asking, the depth of it. The importance to him and his pack. To his wolf. To mine.

He was going to mark me.

Mate me.

Keep me forever.

Not because he had to in order to defeat the moon madness but because he wanted me.

"Do it," I begged, squeezing my core around his cock, practically egging him on. "Claim me."

I didn't even know where the words came from. How I knew to call it that, but again, it sounded right. It *felt* right.

Rob let out a long shaky breath then began with an excruciatingly slow pump, sliding out of me and pushing in, like he was relishing every sensation. He took another slow stroke, but on the third, he slammed in hard and then was off to the races. He fucked me hard, thrusting in hard enough to slap his loins against my smarting ass. My face slid on the covers, and I panted, receiving him, until my own need started to ratchet up to a desperate level.

"Rob," I cried out. "Please!"

Why was he still punishing me? I needed to come. I needed to feel him thicken and hold himself deep. Coat me in his cum. Bite me on the neck. Make me scream and feel like I was his, would always be.

"Willow."

Yes! It felt so good to have him calling my name. The right name this time. He was right there with me. Me!

"Please," I begged again. "Please, I need to come."

"Oh fates," he shouted, releasing my wrists to grasp my nape instead, to hold me immobile, so he could get deeper. Harder.

His thrusts were violent. Wild. Rough.

Perfect.

I screamed.

He roared.

And then he pushed me flat on my belly and sank deep, his hot cum filling my channel as his teeth sank deep into my shoulder.

It didn't hurt. I registered the bite as pleasure. Deep, deep, pleasure.

My orgasm crested, and my legs flailed beneath him, ass squeezed tight, pussy clenched around his girth. I milked his cock of all its cum, moaning and sobbing my release as he filled me.

"Willow?" Rob murmured. His tongue stroked over the wounds in my shoulder. "Willow, angel. Are you okay?"

"Mmm." I couldn't speak, only smiled into the bed, satisfied. Not just physically but mentally too. I was right where I belonged, with Rob and as his mate.

"Willow? Talk to me." He eased out and turned me onto my back beneath him.

I gave him a lazy smile. "I'm perfect," I mumbled. "You've ruined me for all my toys."

A slow, cocky grin spread across his handsome face. "Yes, you are, angel. You're more than perfect." He stroked his thumb down my cheek. "And now you're mine."

"Yes," I agreed. I was. There was nothing between us any longer. No secrets.

"As for those toys, oh, we'll play with them. But you need

to come, you find me, and I'll take care of you. Fingers, mouth, dick. I'm full service."

His gaze dropped to my spread thighs, to his cum I could feel slipping from me.

"I like the sound of that."

His face grew serious, as if he suddenly considered the consequences of his action. "Are you okay with this, Willow?" He kept calling me by name as if testing the sound of it on his tongue. "What about the DEA? You don't have to worry about money, or a job, but I want you happy. Fulfilled."

I made my eyes wider. "Looks like you're moving to Phoenix!"

He went still, like he was considering it.

I smiled at the way he was even sparing a thought about the concept. "I'm kidding. You can't leave your ranch or your pack."

He relaxed.

"I want to stay here with you. Montana is where I grew up. I might not have tons of happy memories about my childhood, but this place... calls to me. I belong here on this land. With you. But having you means I get an entire pack, too. Will they accept me?" I pushed up on my elbows and bit my lip. "I'm not an alpha she-wolf. What happened with that Canadian alpha's daughter anyway?"

The thought of her made me angry, but I was naked here with Rob, his mark on my neck, not on hers.

"I arranged for her to mate with the male she already knew she belonged to. And you are an alpha she-wolf," he said, looking me in the eye and making it very clear he was serious. "Or my wolf wouldn't have picked you. Your human side is irrelevant. I've seen your wolf, and she is magnificent.

No one could deny your power in this pack." He leaned down and kissed me. "It wouldn't matter if they did. I told them all I was mating you, even before I knew you were a shifter. Told them to go to hell if they had a problem with it."

"You did?"

"I went to the Shefield place to tell you. Hell, to throw you over my shoulder and bring you back to the house. My wolf followed your scent and, well... we got a little side-tracked."

My heart filled and overflowed. He'd chosen me just as I chose him.

"I wonder if my wolf would have ever come out if I hadn't been shot," I wondered.

He growled and his jaw clenched at the statement, but he shrugged and ran a finger down the center of my body.

"I told the pack elders off. I chose you, Willow. Human, wolf... giraffe. I'll take you any way I can get you."

I wrapped my arms around his neck and pulled his body down on top of mine. "You did?" I smiled against his lips.

He licked into mine, kissed me thoroughly. "I did, angel. I'd pick you over the pack any day."

I kissed him back. "I would never make you choose." I stared up at his wonderful face. "I'm sorry I lied to you, Rob. I didn't want to, you have to believe that. I couldn't risk you or the case. My hands were tied."

He shook his head. "No, I'm sorry. I was an asshole. You were here on a job, and you couldn't tell me the truth. I get it. You're an incredible agent." He kissed me again. "But please tell me you'll quit. I couldn't fucking stand knowing you might have a gun pointed at your head again."

"I gave notice to Vaughn when I was finishing my reports," I said, and I'd had zero hesitation. "I realized it wasn't my life. Coming here brought me full circle somehow. This is where I belong. Like you said, I was good at my job, but it was just that. A job. I had no life. I do now, with you. With the Wolf pack."

It was true. I think I'd known it from the moment I'd arrived in Cooper Valley, I just hadn't understood it until now.

I was a shifter. I belonged with a pack. And Rob was my alpha.

My pack.

My everything.

30

WILLOW

"YOU READY?" Rob asked. We stood side by side, naked on the porch of the lodge. No one was around for miles.

My pulse raced with excitement. I was going to shift. *Into a wolf!*

Finally.

But right now, I was going to test out my paws. "Ready. Okay, so what do I do?" I asked for the fifteenth time, turning my head to look up at him.

He smiled at me. *Smiled.* Soft, gentle, for once he looked at ease. As if the weight of the world was off his shoulders. As if here, now, with me *was* his world.

"You don't do anything. You just let it happen. Remember how it felt to be a wolf. Bring your awareness to that energy and let go."

I closed my eyes and drew a breath and tried. All I

remembered, though, was my panic. Not understanding what had happened. What I was.

Not until Rob had commanded me to be still.

I opened my eyes. "I remember you did something. To help me shift. You made me do it."

He nodded. "I helped you. An alpha's command is that strong. But you can do it on your own. You don't need my help. You never have. Just be the wolf."

Be the wolf. Right.

I tried again.

Still nothing.

I turned to Rob, sliding my palms over his hairy chest, pressing my breasts up against his ribs. "Please? Make me do it?"

That, too, made sense. My request. I loved when he was in charge. In control. Perhaps my wolf wanted that from him too.

His arm curled around my back, and he pulled me up tight against his body. We hadn't had sex since I'd been shot—he wanted to be sure I healed fully, but he'd promised after I shifted to wolf form once more, the rest of healing would take place.

He squeezed my bare ass in his large palm then released the flesh and slapped. "*Shift.*"

One word.

A command.

In a flash, I was on all fours, looking up at him, then watching him shift, too. Then running together. I laughed—well, the wolf version of laughing—and looked over my shoulder at him. He was right behind me, huge and gray furred, nipping at my flank.

I picked up speed.

It felt *incredible*.

I was so fast! So nimble. I jumped over a fallen log, sailing well above it, way past it. My strength and agility were incredible. I felt... whole. And with Rob by my side, I am safe and protected. As if he was letting me do my thing but would be there if I needed him.

I caught a scent of something interesting. My instincts told me it was a rabbit. I followed it until I found a hole and started digging.

Rob nipped my hind quarters to make me leave it.

I'd probably thank him later, but at the moment, it riled me up. I turned and tussled with him. He quickly dominated me, bringing me to my back and standing over, his jaws loosely caged around my throat. I went slack and gave him my belly, and he let me up, so we could run again.

Submitting to him was as natural and instinctive as breathing.

I ran and ran through the forest, my senses all heightened, my pleasure off the charts. It felt wonderful.

Rob stayed with me as my guard, herding me when he wanted me to change direction, tussling with me when I wanted to play, until at last, he chased me back to the lodge.

He shifted first and stood on the porch, looking down at me.

"You can do it," he encouraged. He wasn't going to command this time. He was going to make me find it on my own.

I brought myself back to the last time. When I'd been lying in the barn, and he'd stroked my fur. What he'd told me then. I closed my eyes, remembered his voice.

And just like that, I found myself crouched on the ground in human form.

"I did it!" I beamed.

"You did." Rob's smile brightened his rugged face. He held his arms out, and I fell into them.

"I love you, Rob Wolf," I said. And I meant it. With all my heart.

He cupped my face. "I love you, Willow Johnson." He cocked his head. "Johnson-Wolf? Or just Willow Wolf?"

I smiled. "Maybe just Willow Wolf. It has a super-hero ring to it, you know?"

He stroked his thumb down my cheek. "Definitely."

EPILOGUE

Rob

New moon pack meetings were formal. Organized. There was a schedule. An agenda. Everyone attended.

Full moon runs happened organically. They weren't required, but they were still tradition. A constancy that every wolf could attend if they wanted to run with others, and they almost always did. Wolves needed to run when the moon was full. There was aggression that had to be let out. Sexual tension. It was unavoidable, especially if unmated and definitely if leaning toward moon madness.

Tonight was the first time I'd run mated. No wildness haunting me. I wanted to run now not out of desperation but out of pleasure.

The mountain was the safe place to roam, so that's where we usually found each other, up in the hills above everyone's homes. We had the pack lodge most started from.

Everyone of shifting age kept a change of clothes there in case that's where they ended up.

Willow and I had arrived early, so she could practice shifting without an audience. The more times she tried, the easier it came, but she'd only done it with me in observance. Having an entire pack watch her, not just because she was a new shifter but because she was my mate, would be daunting. In this freedom, we ran and played. I showed Willow all the best places to roam—my favorite spots.

Eventually we headed back toward the lodge and found most of the pack gathered. The Wolf Ranch shifters—Boyd, Colton, Clint, Rand, Nash, Johnny and Levi—circled up with us right away. Our royal guard, making a horseshoe around us. Willow had not seen anyone else in wolf form and didn't know one from the other. Yet.

The rest of the pack scrambled to assemble as well, many dropping to their bellies to show submission to their mysterious new alpha she-wolf, the beautiful ginger by my side. I waited until they'd all formed a cluster around us, then trotted through them to the lodge, Willow at my side.

We shifted inside and dressed privately, in the bedroom. I wasn't normally shy—shifters were used to being naked around each other, but none of them were going to see my mate's gorgeous body naked. Not without them losing a big hunk of fur from their hind quarters.

Besides it being awkward with my brothers.

When we walked out to join the others, I heard gasps of surprise and whispers like *That's the Shefield girl,* and *I thought she was human.*

Janet was the first to approach, gathering Willow up in her arms. "Well, didn't you surprise us all?" She leaned in to sniff Willow's neck. Willow stared at me over Janet's shoulder, eyes wide. Her hands were at her sides as if she'd never been hugged before. "Your scent has changed. Your shifter DNA just surfaced? Are you a half-breed?"

"Come on, mom, give the female some space," Rand coaxed, throwing a muscled arm around his mother's much smaller shoulders and tossing Willow a wink.

"I'm sorry. I'm just so excited to finally have a daughter." She waved a hand at me and Rand and Clint, Boyd and Colton behind us. "I had all these wonderful boys, two of my own and then the Wolf trio. But now I'm getting daughters. I've got Audrey and Marina... and now Willow. Welcome to the pack, sweetheart." She kissed her cheek. "You're exactly what we needed."

Janet let Willow go, but when she moved to step away, Willow gave her a quick hug of her own. Never knowing a mom, I knew Janet was going to fill that role for her now.

I cleared my throat and the room went silent. Everyone was dying to know what was going on. How I'd ended up mated to this lovely she-wolf who hadn't been a wolf at all just last week. She'd been at the picnic as the Shefield niece and now...

"I'd like to introduce you all to my mate, Willow Johnson. Fate brought her here to me as an undercover agent with the DEA." I set my hand at the back of Willow's neck. It was a show of possession but also of protection. There was no doubt to everyone witnessing that she was mine. "She will be staying on as my mate. I expect you will make her feel welcome."

Excited murmurs rippled through the room and everyone filed forward to offer their welcome and congratulations. I noted they were all here—none of my pack had defected, even knowing I'd planned to mate a human. Not everyone had heard my threat on my porch, but I had no doubt word of it had spread.

Even Nathan Brown came up, tail tucked, throat bared. "Forgive me for questioning your judgement, Alpha," he said. "Looks like it all turned out fine."

I didn't believe he meant the apology, but I didn't care. He knew his place, and while I doubted he'd be any less difficult in the coming years, he wouldn't doubt me again. I had Willow. Everything would be perfect, even if she wasn't a wolf.

I knew my thoughts leaned toward sappy romance and poetry, but hell, I was fucking happy. I'd expected the worst, moon madness to finish me. Alone.

Instead, I had my mate by my side. My parents would have been pleased with Willow. She was strong, independent. Feisty. Brave. Everything to keep me on my toes, just as Mom had with Dad.

I wished they could have met her. Audrey and Marina, too. To know all three Wolf boys were home and leading the pack into the future. With Audrey, one baby at a time.

Tom came over and hugged Willow. "Welcome to the family, Willow. Clint tells me you don't know who your kin is?"

She offered him a smile but shook her head. "That's right. I grew up in foster care here in Montana."

"Here in Montana, hmm?" He rubbed his face. "I'm thinking—ginger wolves are pretty rare. I know a pack that has a streak of ginger near Helena. If you're interested, I could arrange a meeting. Maybe you could find some answers. Up to you, of course."

Her green eyes widened. "Wow. Okay. Yes, I'd like that very much. Thank you, Tom."

He leaned in and gave her a kiss on the cheek. "Anything for our new alpha female." He winked.

I pulled Willow in tight against my side and kissed the top of her head. "You're their new queen, angel. How does that feel?"

She turned and pressed her body against mine, wrapping her arms around my waist and lifting her face to meet my gaze. I saw happiness there, too. We'd been two lost souls that fate brought together. Made us whole in each other.

"It feels right." She nodded her head like she was affirming something important. "Like this is where I belong."

I brushed my lips across hers and held her as if I'd never let go. "That's right, angel. It's exactly where you belong."

Ready for more Wolf Ranch?
Get Wolf Ranch: Savage next!

Pack Rule #4: Guard your pups with your life

We hooked up one night at Cody's Saloon.
The beautiful nurse wanted a ride and I'd given it to her.
Made her scream and sent her home happy.
She didn't tell me there'd been consequences.
She'd kept her secret close. For months.
But what she didn't know could change everything.
That baby she carried wasn't human.
And this wolf would never walk away from his pup.
She may not want me in her life, but that was too bad.

I was moving in—watching over her and providing for my family.

She was under my protection now.

Whether she wanted it or not.

Whether she wanted me or not.

Get Wolf Ranch: Savage!

NOTE FROM VANESSA & RENEE

Guess what? We've got some bonus content for you with Rob and Willow. Yup, there's more!

Click here to read!

WANT FREE RENEE ROSE BOOKS?

Go to http://subscribepage.com/alphastemp to sign up for Renee Rose's newsletter and receive a free copy of *Alpha's Temptation, Theirs to Protect, Owned by the Marine, Theirs to Punish, The Alpha's Punishment, Disobedience at the Dressmaker's* and *Her Billionaire Boss*. In addition to the free stories, you will also get bonus epilogues, special pricing, exclusive previews and news of new releases.

GET A FREE VANESSA VALE BOOK!

Join my mailing list to be the first to know of new releases, free books, special prices and other author giveaways.

http://freeromanceread.com

OTHER TITLES BY RENEE ROSE

Chicago Bratva

"Prelude" in Black Light: Roulette War

The Director

The Fixer

Black Light: Roulette Rematch

The Enforcer

Vegas Underground Mafia Romance

King of Diamonds

Mafia Daddy

Jack of Spades

Ace of Hearts

Joker's Wild

His Queen of Clubs

Dead Man's Hand

Wild Card

More Mafia Romance

Her Russian Master

The Don's Daughter

Mob Mistress

The Bossman

Contemporary

Daddy Rules Series

Fire Daddy

Hollywood Daddy

Stepbrother Daddy

Master Me Series

Her Royal Master

Her Russian Master

Her Marine Master

Yes, Doctor

Double Doms Series

Theirs to Punish

Theirs to Protect

Holiday Feel-Good

Scoring with Santa

Saved

Other Contemporary

Black Light: Valentine Roulette

Black Light: Roulette Redux

Black Light: Celebrity Roulette

Black Light: Roulette War

Black Light: Roulette Rematch

Punishing Portia (written as Darling Adams)

The Professor's Girl

Safe in his Arms

Paranormal

Wolf Ranch Series

Rough

Wild

Feral

Savage

Fierce

Ruthless

Wolf Ridge High Series

Alpha Bully

Alpha Knight

Bad Boy Alphas Series

Alpha's Temptation

Alpha's Danger

Alpha's Prize

Alpha's Challenge

Alpha's Obsession

Alpha's Desire

Alpha's War

Alpha's Mission

Alpha's Bane

Alpha's Secret

Alpha's Prey

Alpha's Sun

Alpha's Moon

Midnight Doms

Alpha's Blood

His Captive Mortal

Alpha Doms Series

The Alpha's Hunger

The Alpha's Promise

The Alpha's Punishment

Other Paranormal

The Winter Storm: An Ever After Chronicle

Sci-Fi

Zandian Masters Series

His Human Slave

His Human Prisoner

Training His Human

His Human Rebel

His Human Vessel

His Mate and Master

Zandian Pet

Their Zandian Mate

His Human Possession

Zandian Brides

Night of the Zandians

Bought by the Zandians

Mastered by the Zandians

Zandian Lights

Kept by the Zandian

Claimed by the Zandian

Stolen by the Zandian

Other Sci-Fi

The Hand of Vengeance

Her Alien Masters

Regency

The Darlington Incident

Humbled

The Reddington Scandal

The Westerfield Affair

Pleasing the Colonel

Western

His Little Lapis

The Devil of Whiskey Row

The Outlaw's Bride

Medieval

Mercenary

Medieval Discipline

Lords and Ladies

The Knight's Prisoner

Betrothed

Held for Ransom

The Knight's Seduction

The Conquered Brides (5 book box set)

Renaissance

Renaissance Discipline

ALSO BY VANESSA VALE

For the most up-to-date listing of my books, go to:

vanessavalebooks.com

All Vanessa Vale titles are available at Apple, Google, Kobo, Barnes & Noble, Amazon and other retailers worldwide.

ABOUT RENEE ROSE

USA TODAY BESTSELLING AUTHOR RENEE ROSE loves a dominant, dirty-talking alpha hero! She's sold over a half million copies of steamy romance with varying levels of kink. Her books have been featured in USA Today's *Happily Ever After* and *Popsugar*. Named Eroticon USA's Next Top Erotic Author in 2013, she has also won *Spunky and Sassy's* Favorite Sci-Fi and Anthology author, *The Romance Reviews* Best Historical Romance, and *Spanking Romance Reviews'* Best Sci-fi, Paranormal, Historical, Erotic, Ageplay and favorite couple and author. She's hit the *USA Today* list five times with various anthologies.

Please follow her on:
Bookbub | Goodreads

Renee loves to connect with readers!

www.reneeroseromance.com
reneeroseauthor@gmail.com

ABOUT VANESSA VALE

Vanessa Vale is the *USA Today* bestselling author of sexy romance novels, including her popular Bridgewater historical series and hot contemporary romances. With over one million books sold, Vanessa writes about unapologetic bad boys who don't just fall in love, they fall hard. Her books are available worldwide in multiple languages in e-book, print, audio and even as an online game. When she's not writing, Vanessa savors the insanity of raising two boys and figuring out how many meals she can make with a pressure cooker. While she's not as skilled at social media as her kids, she loves to interact with readers.

BookBub

Instagram

facebook.com/vanessavaleauthor

twitter.com/iamvanessavale

instagram.com/vanessa_vale_author

bookbub.com/profile/vanessa-vale

Printed in Great Britain
by Amazon

85791385R00139